NEW
BLOOD

The hot, dusty, garbage-strewn streets of Harlem seem more depressing than ever to Imamu Jones after his recent stay with foster-parents in Brooklyn. He has drifted away from his old friends and is glad when two new guys, Pierre and Olivette, move in around the block, volunteering to help him refurbish his mother's run-down apartment.

Handsome, super-cool, intelligent, Olivette becomes a close friend, but there is something about him that troubles Imamu. Could it be that the newcomer is too perfect to be true?

But soon other sinister events take up Imamu's attention. Iggy, a teenage murderer, is released from jail, and Imamu and Olivette are hauled in by the police, who accuse them of a series of mysterious 'phantom' burglaries. Released on bail, the two boys team up to try and solve the case themselves, only to find the evidence points ever closer to home . . .

More than an exciting thriller, this sequel to *The Disappearance* paints a grimly realistic, yet sympathetic, picture of life in an inner city where violence and prejudice thrive.

Rosa Guy was born in Trinidad. Orphaned at a young age, she grew up on the streets of New York. Her first choice of artistic expression was the theatre; however, frustrated by the prejudice that existed, she turned her talents to writing. For over twenty years she has written a great number of internationally acclaimed books, including *The Friends*, *The Disappearance* and *Edith Jackson*. She is twice married, has a son and four grand-children, and still lives in New York.

Other books by Rosa Guy

THE DISAPPEARANCE
THE FRIENDS
RUBY
EDITH JACKSON
PARIS, PEE WEE AND BIG DOG

ROSA GUY

NEW GUYS AROUND THE
BLOCK

PUFFIN BOOKS

PUFFIN BOOKS

Published by the Penguin Group
Penguin Books Ltd, 27 Wrights Lane, London W8 5TZ, England
Penguin Books USA Inc., 375 Hudson Street, New York, New York 10014, USA
Penguin Books Australia Ltd, Ringwood, Victoria, Australia
Penguin Books Canada Ltd, 10 Alcorn Avenue, Toronto, Ontario, Canada M4V 3B2
Penguin Books (NZ) Ltd, 182–190 Wairau Road, Auckland 10, New Zealand

Penguin Books Ltd, Registered Offices: Harmondsworth, Middlesex, England

First published in the USA by Delacorte Press 1983
First published in Great Britain by Victor Gollancz 1983
Published in Penguin Books 1989
Reissued in Puffin Books 1995
1 3 5 7 9 10 8 6 4 2

Copyright © Rosa Guy, 1983
All rights reserved

Printed in England by Clays Ltd, St Ives plc

To my friends
Joan and Evelyn
and to
Dedier, Chief, and Avatar

1

Packed together, they pushed, shoved, straining toward the round spot of light—and escape. Blocking their retreat, the shadow stretched out over them, threatening oblivion. They squeezed, clawed, fought each other, stampeding forward. Neck to neck, fur brushing fur, bodies glistening in the wild scramble.

Rats! Hundreds and hundreds of rats! Rats locked together in a frenzied struggle—mindless, snapping, desperate. And he was one of them. He could see his eyes. They were intelligent. He didn't belong. Opening his mouth he shouted, *"Squeak, squeak, squeak."* His back bristled—and then he fought. Fighting the pack, fighting to move backward, fighting to stand still . . . Digging his claws into the wood of the floor, he cowered, still resisting the mob. But the surge of terrified gray bodies kept pushing, sweeping him along.

Intelligently, he began to maneuver forward. He shouldered his way, first past one, then another, burrowing through one.group, then another. And he made it. Haloed by the spot of light, he jumped—into space!

Floating down, his paws clawing the air, bodies falling

on either side of him, he looked down. Water raged
below, beating against jagged rocks on which hundreds
of gray, furry cadavers had already been pierced, blood
darkening the water. . . .

Jumping out of bed in the hot room, Imamu switched
on the light at the side of his bed and rushed to the
dresser. Staring into the mirror, he ran his hands over his
face. Yes, he still stood six feet two, smooth, black, and
slender. His Afro haircut, matted down from sleep, made
a crown around his head—rough, instead of slick to the
touch. He pinched his nose; it was high, broad instead of
pointed. And his hands—praise the Lord—were still
large, the fingers long. "Imamu Jones, you're still a
human goddamn being. . . ."

He sat at the edge of his bed, fighting for control.
Picking up a soiled shirt from the chair next to the bed,
he wiped the sweat from his clammy body. The clock on
the dresser pointed to five-thirty. Easing away from the
cold spot of his sweat, Imamu got back into bed.
"Imamu Jones," he whispered, "what in the world did
you do to earn yourself that nightmare, man?" He lay
staring up at the ceiling, at the paint curling as though
ready to fall on him.

He turned his eyes to the window, looked long and
hard at the torn shade, the dirty curtains, then at the
walls—gray from years of neglect, the cracked plaster
spilling fine dust over the floors. He gazed at the black
finger marks around the doorknob. And all through the
house it was the same—the kitchen, its walls thick with
grease; the bathroom a nightmare of peeling ceiling and
walls; his mother's bedroom, the hallway, crying out for
paint. . . .

"Tomorrow," he whispered again. "No—this very day —when I get up . . ."

He had promised himself, on the day he had taken his mother to the hospital, that if her life were spared, he would bring her back to a home worth coming to. He had promised her, when she had regained consciousness, that if she stayed in the hospital for the cure, she would never feel like taking another drink again. And he had started off okay. He had cleared out her room, thrown out all the empty wine bottles that had accumulated in the corners. He had taken all the dirty clothes, including the sheets from the beds, and had washed them. He had thrown out the jars they had been using for glasses, had bought new cups, a few plates. But the scraping, the painting—the real hard work—he kept putting off. At first the excuse had been he was looking for work. But there were no jobs to be found out there. Going to Brooklyn to see Gail wasn't getting anything done.

He really needed some help. Who did he have? Fur-gerson? The dude was so lazy. . . . Still, if not Furgie, who? He used to have so many friends around Harlem. Now only one person came to mind. Furgie. "And all this work . . . ?"

Imamu turned over on his stomach, pulled the sheet over his head, then heard, "Squeak, squeak" . . . from beneath the bed. He sat up. "Today," he promised. "This very day—I'll block every rat hole, and start painting. That is a promise or my name ain't Imamu Jones." Then, pulling the sheet over his head, he fell asleep.

And then he woke late. It was noon when he stepped out on his stoop, squinted in the glare of the July sun, and remembered he and Gail were supposed to go to Far

Rockaway beach. On such a hot, clear day what would
be better? He hated breaking a date with Gail. Between
sitting for hours in the unemployment office, waiting for
the never-never job, and visiting his mother in the hospital, the times he spent with his foster sister-girl friend
had been too short and too far between. Now it was
already late for the ride out to Brooklyn. Imamu looked
around the hot street. Depressing. He took a toothpick
out of his shirt pocket and stuck it in his mouth, looking
down toward 135th Street, then up toward 136th, then
into the building directly across the street from him.

It was partially abandoned. On the upper floors the
windows were all broken out. On the lower floors, where
a few tenants still lived, many of the windows had been
boarded up with cardboard; through others, heads were
stuck out, looking at the busy street. The buildings on
both sides of the one where Imamu lived had already
been reduced to shells, stripped of everything, and were
falling in on themselves. Farther up the avenue, and
down—except for the building that housed the pool hall,
with its offices above—they were the same. The neighborhood had always been dilapidated. Now it was dis-
aster.

Leaving the stoop, Imamu walked to the corner, deliberately looking away from the winos—his mother's old
cronies—and the addicts sitting in the scooped-out buildings, from the children running into the shells and out
into the garbage-strewn streets. Had he always hated it
so much? Or had living for that short time in the Brooklyn brownstone of his foster parents made it appear so
much worse? When had this total collapse started? Why
hadn't he noticed it until he came back to the neighborhood?

Biting hard on his toothpick, Imamu headed for the corner, then stood looking toward the park—St. Nicholas Park, two short blocks away, parched, its boulders gray, glinting beneath the harsh light of the sun, sparse grass barely visible on the rocky slopes. Beneath the boulders, near the entrance of the subway, drunks sat in the shade of skimpy trees, their bodies suggesting an argument in full swing.

Imamu moved toward the corner telephone booth, although he knew that its coin box had long ago been ripped out and the receiver dangled uselessly. Only a miracle would have had the telephone company replace it, but habit forced him to look in.

Why had he come back to all of this? His mother. No regrets. What if he hadn't been there when she had fallen into her drunken coma? That would have been the end of her—and of weakness, of hope, of life. . . .

"Hey, Imamu, my man—what about letting me hold a coin . . . ?" Butler stood beside Imamu, his restless eyes trying to look cool. Imamu let his face go hard, his eyes flat. "See me working? I'm out here too, you know?"

"That the way you treat your old buddy, buddy?"

"Ain't got it." Imamu stood at the phone booth watching Butler walk away to stand in front of a bombed-out shell of a building, where Babs, his girl, sat on a concrete slab, pulling a pair of panties on their four-year-old son.

Babs had been pretty once—brown skin, light brown curly hair, and a shapely body. Imamu had had eyes for her. But her one aim in life had been to keep Butler—who had been a big time break-and-enter man—straight. Now they both were skinny and strung out. Babs was only eighteen.

She looked over at Imamu, her eyes half-closed, her

mouth pulled down, a cigarette stuck in one corner, smoke drifting over her eyes. She nodded at him. "Hey, baby, you turning my old man down. Junior's got to have milk."

"It's against the law to make counterfeit," Imamu answered. "And my one aim in life is to stay out of jail."

So many of Imamu's friends were strung out on drugs, in jail for stealing, or dead from ODs. It hurt. But he couldn't cry forever. Give one dime to Butler and the word would go around that Mrs. Jones's VA check had come. Addicts would crawl up the walls to get into his place. Clean him out. It had happened before. Junkies didn't have friends, they only had needs.

Al Stacy, standing in his usual place in front of the pool room, collecting numbers and talking to a group of the guys, saw Imamu as he headed toward him. He broke off talking to call out, "Hey, Youngblood, this talk's for you, too."

"Be with you," Imamu called back, going inside to the telephone from where he could see Al Stacy through the glass, draped impressively in his white summer suit and white hat, he dialed.

The phone rang once. "Hello." Gail's silky voice in his ear gave him instant misery because he had called to disappoint her. He could see her where she stood at the phone—slim, long brown legs shining out of short shorts, her hair braided in thin corn rows falling about her shoulders. Gail loved short shorts—and he loved the look of her in them.

"Hello, beat of my body," Imamu said, teasing, because it was true.

"Imamu Jones, where are you? Why aren't you here? Do you know what time it is?"

"I know. I know. Look, Gail, I can't make it. . . ."

"Your mother . . . ?"

"No, the apartment. . . ." He hated telling her he got up too late. "I got to get with it."

"Today? What's wrong with tomorrow? I have lunch all fixed."

Imamu squinted out at the hot sky. God, he wanted to be with her, even if only on her tree-lined street, out of sight of bombed-out buildings, the nightmare. It seemed so strange that it had been a year since he had lived on that street—almost that long since he had moved back. "I hate to disappoint you—but I can't just keep putting it off. . . ."

"I'll put the lunch away and come to help. . . ."

"Gail, I got to do this myself," he said. "You know how I feel about that?"

"But, Imamu, I'll be leaving for Jamaica next week. . . ."

Regret that he had spoken so decisively filled Imamu. He wanted to change his mind but Gail kept on. "Okay, this time. But when I get back I want it to be finished. I won't stand any more excuses—promise?"

"Promise," Imamu said, holding on to his decision. "I'm getting started right away."

Imamu kept looking for Furgerson, as he talked to Gail. He wasn't in the group around Al Stacy. He was too big to be missed.

"When will you be back?"

"In a few weeks."

"A few weeks? That long. . . ."

"I'm just giving you time," Gail said.

Hanging up the telephone, Imamu went outside and skirted the group of young men talking to Al. Still not seeing Furgerson, he went to lean against a car parked at the curb.

Al Stacy broke off his talk to say: "Hey, Youngblood, lean off the hardware."

"Sorry, man," Imamu said, jerking away from the black Cadillac.

"It's okay," Al Stacy joked. "We all make mistakes." A ripple of laughter broke the serious mood of the guys he was talking to. But Al Stacy intended to keep them serious.

"I hope you hear what I am saying," he said. "The Man don't be caring about you studs beating on black folks' head, or ripping old black folks off their loot. But he won't have you messing with white folks. If you—whosoever it is—keep it up, the Man will get you! Track you down! Ain't no way you gonna hide. . . ."

Taking out his silk handkerchief to wipe his brown face, Al Stacy looked like a throwback to old times beside the jean-wearing dudes and the black-suited Muslims. He hitched up his shoulders so that his jacket fell smoothly onto his tight stomach and looked around with a half sneer that seemed to be looking down despite his shortness.

"Brother Stacy," Omar, a dedicated Muslim—tall, thin, in his black wool suit—stopped him. "Why do you speak of this to us?"

"I ain't saying you, man. I ain't asking who. Don't want to know. I'm just warning you guys—that's all."

"Brother Stacy." Omar kept at him. "The reason you're warning us is because you suspect one of us. Why do you feel that this burglarizing of those white folks' apartments has to do with us?"

"Because those blue hound dogs picked up the scent

in Harlem—and to be more exact, around this neighborhood. Them hounds been up and down this avenue asking questions, taking names. . . ."

"And who's giving them names, Brother Stacy?"

"It ain't me," Al Stacy answered. "Like I say, I don't know. I'm just saying whoever—stop."

"Oh so, Brother Stacy, you feel you're required to do the police work for them. . . ."

An uncomfortable shuffling of feet spoke of a feeling that Al Stacy's lectures might be a cover. Suspicion never died on a street where nobody was trusted. Folks still trusted Al Stacy. But Omar took his religion and his nationalism seriously. When he brought up something, even nonbelievers listened. Omar had been one of the guys Imamu had hung with—he and Muhammed—when their names had been Dan, Joe, and John. They had become Muslims together. And outside an occasional lifting of snack foods from shops for their "nourishment of mind and body," they'd never messed around. And then the shopkeeper Fein was killed, which had nothing to do with them and everything to do with the non-Muslim Iggy. Crazy Iggy who had pulled a gun and shot Fein, landing Muhammed and Iggy in jail. Imamu had ended up in a foster home with the Aimsleys, and it was the end of their brand of Islam. But Omar had gone deep into religion and black nationalism.

"I ain't doing no police work," Al Stacy was protesting. "But I'll be damn if I want them coming around this avenue messing with business."

"Then what you're saying, Brother Stacy, is that the police is making things tough for you. It's not our heads you be caring about. It's your bread."

"I ain't apologizing," Al Stacy said, hitching up his

shoulders to readjust his jacket. His eyes had gone cold, mean. "But now you said it, no—I don't want my hustle being messed over."

"Tough," Omar said. "And I don't want no hand-kerchief-head hustler trying to endear himself with the law to be warning me about nothing."

"And I won't stand back and let any two-by-four crook making a dirty trail that leads the bulls right to me—see?"

But the cops knew what Al Stacy was about. They could bust him any time—he didn't pay off. It had to be that they were hard-pressed for answers to give him a hard time.

"Dirty trails been leading them to this avenue—if they wanted to see it," Omar said, nodding to a white custom-built convertible driving by. A murmur went through the crowd. All eyes turned to see the car with its Rolls-Royce front and its Lincoln Continental back, slowing down to a stop before Imamu's building. It was immediately surrounded by junkies, who had come crawling from the bombed-out buildings like ants. They followed Stuff Smith, the pusher, and his white boss, the dealer, when they got out of the car and went into the building across the street from the pool hall. Automatically, Imamu's eyes looked toward the imposing, silent police station in the middle of the next block. He looked back as Al Stacy said:

"That's something else. The President of the United States and God up above can't do nothing about that. And nobody else is about to try. I'm just talking about me, see . . . ?"

But Omar's suspicion had broken Al Stacy's hold on

the crowd. They started moving away. Imamu, too. He had seen Furgerson, standing at the corner, talking to two strange guys.

"Hey Furgie," Imamu called, going toward them. "I been looking for you. Didn't you say you would help me when I got ready to do up the house?"

"Yeah," Furgerson said, eyeing Imamu.

"Well, I'm ready."

"Not on the hottest day of the year," Furgerson said. Furgerson was one of the few people Imamu knew who had never been on drugs, religion, or gangs. He had always been too busy eating. And he showed it. His shirt pulled out of his pants, and buttons had popped off, leaving his stomach partly exposed. His heavy feet ran down the backs of his shoes. His round face, the skin pushed out, shone with oil and sweat.

"It's got to be today."

"How come?"

"Because I . . ." It was impossible to tell Furgerson it was because of a nightmare—or that he had promised Gail. So he said, "My old lady, man—she'll be out soon. . . ."

"Tomorrow?"

"Naw—but I got to start sometime. She's been in two weeks . . ."

"What say the day after tomorrow?"

"Why then?"

"Radio said another hot day. . . ."

"Look, Furgie . . ."

"Why don't you be taking one of them long trips to Brooklyn. You do most days . . . ?"

Imamu knew that Furgerson had been angry because

he had gone to see Gail, one time, when Furgerson had
wanted to hang out. "Man, I ain't been going to Brooklyn that much. I been looking for work."

"That what they call it?" Furgerson said, smirking.

Imamu wanted to get angry but didn't dare to. He
turned to the boys Furgerson had been talking to. Good-
looking boys. Brothers, Imamu guessed because of their
general resemblance. They were the same complexion—
light tan. The older of the two—a youth about nineteen
—had deep-set golden-brown eyes and stood almost six
feet, with broad chest and shoulders. The younger—thir-
teen—was about five eight, fragile, poetic-looking with
wide green eyes too large for his delicate face. Imamu
studied the older boy, liking him—the way his deep eyes
darkened with his I-like-you smile.

Imamu waited to be introduced. Instead, Furgerson,
his fat shoulders twitching, kept trying out excuses.
"Every day, the minute you leave your house, you can't
wait, making that A train, hot-tailing it. Brooklyn, here
I comes. Try to talk to you—but no, not when it's
Brooklyn time. Now, all of a sudden, you want . . .
a hell of a friend, I say. Well, I got to get me a job,
too. . . ."

The furthest thing from Furgie's mind was to find
work. Imamu knew that. "Furgie, look, I'll buy the food,
man—anything you want . . ."

"Hey you guys. . . ." Al Stacy called out to them. "I
got talk for you two. . . ."

"Furgerson," the older boy said. "We must go.
Mother—you know? Be in touch tomorrow?"

"Okay, will do." Furgerson waved them on and stood
watching as they crossed the avenue, going uptown.

"Who are they?" Imamu asked as he and Furgerson walked toward Al Stacy.

"Friends. They like to hang with me—dig?"

"Known them long?"

"No—only a couple of weeks. They're new guys around the block. . . ."

2

Furgerson had to be two hundred pounds, every one of them slow. He seemed to be falling apart with the hot weather, the reason he gave for not finding work. Actually he didn't need to work. His mother had a good job as a nurse in the hospital and didn't mind looking after her only boy. She even managed to shop for clothes that actually fit.

"Hi, Al Stacy." Furgerson walked up to the gambler, holding out a dollar bill. "What about six sixty-four today. And I don't want change."

Al Stacy took the bill, looked on both sides of it, wrote Furgerson's number on his thumbnail and pocketed the bill. "You can't be expecting to get rich like this?" he said.

"Give me time, man. I'm only eighteen."

"You got it," Al answered. "All the time and space you need. You're a growing boy."

"And you ain't funny," Furgerson said.

"Get him, Al Stacy," Imamu said, pushing for an advantage. "This joker promised to help me paint, and now he's reneging on the deal."

"Paint? You mean work? Imamu, I took you for smart," Al Stacy said, laughing. "The only work this sucker will do will be bending his elbow. Why don't you buy a ham and bring it to your joint? He'll be there."

"You still ain't funny," Furgerson said. "But you trying. Might make it yet. But for real, I got to get a job 'fore my ma puts me out. I'd have been in the employment office if I hadn't been taking those two new guys around."

"Who're they?" Al Stacy asked.

"Nice guys. And their mother . . ." Furgerson covered his face with his hands and shook the fat on his body. "Oh my God, why didn't someone tell me that women like her existed?" He made waves with his hand. "She is the most . . ."

"I hope she's over twenty and built like a tank, or you'll never make it," Al Stacy teased.

"With a lady like that, man—age or weight can't count."

"Ain't no way to be talking about folks' old ladies," Imamu said, flushing. And at Furgerson's surprise, added, "Come on, Furgie, what you say? You gonna help me out?"

"How much you paying me?"

"Pay? You got to be joking. I ain't even got enough to buy paint."

"Then what you want from me, man?" Furgerson asked. "How you expect me to do my heavy courting if I ain't got clothes what fits?"

"When your old lady be coming home?" Al Stacy asked Imamu.

"Dunno. A couple of weeks. But I got to start on the joint if I want to finish before she do."

"A couple of weeks? And you ain't got enough for paint?"

"Like I said. Her VA check came—but after rent, light, man. . . . And I swear I been looking for work. Ain't found a thing. . . ." Imamu had been taking care of his mother's checks since he had come back from the Aimsleys in the fall. It stopped her from using it all on wine or getting ripped off on the street.

"How you expect to get the place fixed if you ain't got loot, man," Al Stacy asked.

"A li'l here and a li'l there," Imamu said. "Beats doing nothing."

"Save her VA checks for when she gets home." Al Stacy pulled a roll of bills from his pocket, peeled off a fifty, and pushed it against Imamu. "Buy yourself some paint."

"Man," Furgerson said, his eyes wide. "You can buy more than paint with that. You can buy a mess of ham— and grits. . . ."

Imamu moved away from the bill in the gambler's hand. "What I do to deserve that?"

"You didn't, Youngblood. Your old lady did. Did you know she give me the first five-dollar bill to feed myself when I first come up north? Yeah—she helped me over some hard times. . . ." He looked away, down the street, remembering, then back at Imamu. "A grand lady, Mrs. Jones. It had to be hard on her losing your old man in Vietnam," he said. "That pushed her right over the top. Lord, she was sure crazy about that man. . . . Tell you one thing, Youngblood, there never was a better lady walking down these streets—that avenue. . . ."

Al Stacy remembered. Imamu remembered her too,

a gentle, sweet-talking, brave lady. She had been real brave, struggling at his side to save Iggy from the burning apartment downstairs. They had inhaled so much smoke trying to break the lock to save him. Iggy's mother had locked him in. Women did some strange things to keep their kids off the streets.

He had given his mother some tough times too, Imamu thought as he felt Al Stacy's hand, still pushing the bill against his chest. He took it. "Thanks, man. . . ." Al Stacy shrugged. He knew that Imamu was thanking him as much for the memory as the money.

"Hey, man, what's the talk you got. . . ." Furgerson asked Al.

"Talk . . . ? Oh yeah. . . . Your boy's getting out— soon."

"Boy? What boy? Getting out? From where?"

"Iggy."

"Iggy!" Imamu and Furgerson almost shouted. Then Imamu asked. "Where'd you hear that lie from?"

"The vine, man. Seems Muhammed confessed that he done old man Fein in—so they letting Iggy out."

"But that ain't true," Imamu protested. "Muhammed didn't. Iggy did it. I was there. I saw it."

"But you clammed, remember?"

"I didn't have to talk. Iggy confessed hisself."

"See? Now Muhammed confessed and Iggy gets free."

"Why?" Imamu asked, confused. "Why would Muhammed do a thing like that?"

"Can't prove a thing by me," Al Stacy said, putting his hand in his pockets and shrugging his shoulders to adjust his jacket over his flat stomach. "Muhammed's dead. . . ."

"Muhammed! Dead? How?"

"Knife in the gut."

"That's Iggy's doing," Furgerson said, fear causing his fat body to move restlessly.

"You don't know that," Imamu said. "We don't know that."

But even as he defended him, Iggy's set face with its close-set eyes, its inverted forehead, haunted Imamu. A knife was Iggy's tool and had been since he was eight. Imamu had seen Iggy rip open the bellies of many a stray cat and dog with one move of his gleaming blade.

"He got to go before the judge—some such thing," Al Stacy said. "But you got that? That addle-brain son of a female dog what needs to be in a nuthouse—out here walk . . ." He broke off as Gladys Dawson turned the corner and walked toward them.

"Hey, baby doll," he said, his voice changing from bitter to sweet. "What's the prettiest, sexiest chick in New York doing this fine day . . . ?"

Gladys could turn on the gleam in the gambler's eyes from two miles away. He had dug her since she was a sexy twelve, and he a man in his thirties. Now, he had to be in his forties and she eighteen, but the light kept glowing.

"Hey," she greeted them, her eyes going over Imamu. "Ain't nothin' to me as you can see."

"More to you than meets anybody's eyes," Al Stacy said, looking her up and down.

She wore a white dress that came over her plump knees, showing off heavy, well-shaped legs; a halter top exposed a stretch of smooth black back, shining shoulders, and her thick, muscled arms. Gladys tossed her head for them to get a good look at her new wet curly

look. "Hey, lover boy." She flashed bold black eyes at
Imamu. "Where you been holing up?"

"Some hairstyle you got there, girl," Imamu said.

"You like it?" Gladys smiled at him.

"Boss—boss," Imamu said. Then, to show his distance from her, he waved to Al Stacy. "Got to make it,
man. . . ."

Imamu and Furgerson turned the corner, going up the
avenue. Strange how in their dwindling space of crumbling buildings and growing numbers of drug addicts, the
release of one seventeen-year-old could threaten what
was left. They crossed the street, walking past the newsstand that sold everything from bubble gum to hairpins,
nodding to the old news vendor, gnarled as an old tree
that had braved too many storms. They crossed the avenue in front of the supermarket, ambling down to Furgerson's street—their hang-out street now—before Furgerson said:

"What time you want me by tomorrow, man?"

Blackmail. Imamu knew that's what was behind Furgerson's offer. Furgerson needed his protection because
Imamu was Iggy's "boy." He had been since way back
when he had helped save Iggy's life. Nevertheless, he
accepted.

"Early, man. I'll buy the paint now but let's get to it
tomorrow before the sun—"

"Wait up, you two." Gladys's high heels clicked behind them. Coming alongside, she grabbed Imamu's arm.
"What's your hurry? Ain't seen you in months, Imamu
Jones, and no sooner I catch up with you, you go rushing
off. Where you been keeping?"

They turned the corner into the block and stood before the apartment building where Furgerson and Gladys lived.

"Around," Imamu answered, taking out a toothpick and putting it in his mouth. The street was lined with brownstones and trees, making it one of the nice remaining streets.

"Around where?" Gladys asked. "I been wanting you to take me to the new East Side Disco."

"I keeps busy, Gladys," Imamu said.

"Yeah—seeing that bitch."

"Hold it, Gladys, you know I don't like—"

"Who gives a damn what you likes? That snooty heifer you been . . ."

Imamu jerked his arm away. Then, worried that Gladys might use her thick fists, he grabbed them. Gladys liked to swing out. She didn't need much encouragement. "Gladys, please don't be talking about my lady. You don't know her." Gladys had seen Gail once, when Gail came uptown to see Imamu.

"Lady!" Gladys snorted. "If that chick's a lady, what am I?"

Imamu laughed, shaking his head. He liked Gladys and didn't want to quarrel with her. He respected her because she had come up the hard way—on the streets. And while her two brothers had gone on junk, she was working in McDonald's in the Bronx to support her mother. Imamu was and would always be her friend. But no matter how many dudes Gladys went out with, she kept thinking that their young days of teasing and kissing in the hallways and on roofs had hooked them together for life.

"You're one fine chick," Imamu said. "Ask Al Stacy. He's been big-eyeing you all these years."

"What sewer-picker ask you to choose my men for me?" Gladys said. She cultivated dirty scenes, like weeds, to flash past the mind, without a thought, or care, of whom it might hurt. "I picks the garbage I wants to eat, Imamu Jones. I don't need no old men what needs crutches to get it up—know what I mean?"

"Right, you don't," Imamu agreed. "I'll tell the world. You can pick any number you wants."

"Yeah—and I'm ready to pick one right here and now. When do we get together, Imamu?"

"But I ain't garbage, baby."

"You are—only the dessert kind—what say tomorrow?"

"Tomorrow it is," Imamu said. "Bright and early. Furgerson is supposed to be coming to the house at sunrise. I'm buying the paint right now. Say, Gladys, you got a good brush you can bring with you?"

"You got to be kidding." Gladys put her hand on her hips and tapped a foot. "Is that what you want from me? You don't need me. You need that sweet-faced, Brooklyn whore. That's who you need—or do you think she's too good. . . ." Snatching away as Imamu tried to pinch her cheek, she marched into the building, her high heels clicking, her plump thighs shaking.

3

". . . no clues have as yet been found in the case known
as—for want of a better name—the Phantom Burglar. . . .
When does he come? When does he leave? This is the
question the police are trying to decide. . . . All that is
known is that sometime, during the day—or night—the
Phantom enters apartments in the most secure areas—
first, in Harlem, then Morningside Heights—and seems
to be working his way farther downtown on Fifth Avenue."

A chunk of ceiling broke off and fell on Imamu's
head, crumbling and sending chips into his eyes. With a
curse, Imamu jumped down from his mother's dresser
and reached around, wth his eyes closed, until his hand
came in contact with the bed. Grabbing the sheet, he
wiped his face, then stood at the mirror trying to get the
chip from his eye.

He had started without waiting for Furgerson. Now he
wondered if he had been wise. Looking up at the ceiling,
he had to admit that he hadn't made much progress. He
sat on the dresser, letting his feet dangle, gazing up at the
small area of the ceiling he had scraped. Then he looked

at the gallon cans of paint he had bought. They were unopened. A feeling of helplessness came over him.

"This . . . burglar, leaves no clues. The police seem to think that the culprit—or culprits—are nonprofessionals and that they might be from Harlem. . . ." Annoyed by the continual news on the radio, Imamu left the dresser to change to music. Instead, he turned off the radio and went to the window, where he stood staring out—first at the broken windows across from him, then down to the street where the junkies and winos sat at the edges of the caves away from the rays of the sun, then at the garbage drying up in the street, from the heat of another hot day.

He thought of calling the work off and going to call Gail. Why not go to the beach? What better day? But he heard Gail's voice loud and clear: "Are you finished already?" If he said yes, she would say, "Good, I'll come up to see. . . ." If he said no, she'd get real quiet, and guilt would rise unsettling, the way it had when they talked about his going back to school and he never starting. If he said, "I changed my mind—the dump looks better as is," her silence would go on and on—all through him, messing with his self-confidence. Anyway, she'd be packing to leave for Jamaica. He'd only be in her way. . . .

"Big, fat, lazy . . ." he whispered at Furgerson who crossed his mind, "liar, liar—a damn liar. . . ." Leaving the window, he climbed back onto the dresser. And then the bell rang.

He looked at the clock, in the kitchen, as he rushed down the hall. Eleven o'clock. The sucker really had a nerve. Yanking the door open, he shouted, "Where the hell have you been? It's about time. . . ." Then stood staring open-mouthed at the two boys who had been with Furgerson the day before.

They stared back, as surprised at Imamu's outburst as he was to see them at his door. Seconds passed, then the older boy said, "I do hope working together doesn't mean we must abuse each other."

"Sorry, man," Imamu said, stepping aside. "Thought it was Furgie."

"Isn't he here yet? I came earlier than I promised. I rarely ever leave my house before noon. . . ."

"Oh?" Imamu said, because he couldn't think of anything else to say.

"My name is Olivette. Olivette Larouche."

"Olivette?" Imamu said stupidly, then: "Oh, Oh, I'm Imamu. . . ."

"I know." The handsome boy smiled. "And this is Pierre—my younger brother, Pierre Larouche."

Pierre's wide, green, begging eyes brought a rush of instant affection. Imamu reached out and tousled his curly, reddish hair. "Hey, Shorty," he said. "Hiya doin'?"

"I said his name was Pierre," Olivette said.

Imamu's eyebrows raised in surprise. Then after a moment's glance into the deep-set golden-brown eyes, he surprised himself even more by saying, "Hello—Pierre." He extended his hand to the younger boy.

"Hiya doin'," Pierre said, the anxious look on his face showing his embarrassment. Immediately Imamu felt a bond between them, and as they walked down the hallway, Pierre in front, managed to maneuver himself between them.

Olivette seemed not to notice. "Furgerson said you needed help, Imamu," he said. "What have you done so far?"

They entered Imamu's mother's room and stood looking around. Olivette looked up at the ceiling where Imamu had been working; then they followed him into the adjoining never-lived-in living room. Next, Olivette left them to go down the hall, stopping first to glance into the kitchen, before going back to Imamu's room and the bathroom. And all the while Imamu sensed Pierre's anxiety at his reaction.

"This will never do, you know," Olivette said when he came back. "Where is your canvas—your newspapers? How can you work like this? The entire apartment will be a wreck by the time you're finished. . . . You do have newspapers . . . ?"

Deliberately taking a toothpick out of his shirt pocket, Imamu picked his teeth, waiting for his resentment to subside. He hadn't decided how to answer when the doorbell rang, bringing him down the hall. And he walked slowly, as he went to let Furgerson in.

"Man, am hon-gry." Furgerson pushed past Imamu and waddled down the hall, his fat frame filling it.

"Where the hell you been?" Imamu barked, letting his anger out on him.

"The police, man. They trying to give us straight guys a hard time on these long, hot summer days. They stopped a bunch of us. Frisked us, talking about us knowing more than we telling—garbage like that. . . . I told 'em—talking 'bout a phantom burglar, I said. Big as I am, how'n the hell can I get in or out of a place without somebody seeing me? I ain't no magician. . . ." He went into the kitchen and opened the empty refrigerator.

"Man, you ain't got one thing in this box. What do I eat?"

"In this house folks starts off working—and that goes for you too—before you eat."

"How'm I gonna work?" Furgerson said, his voice falsetto. "I ain't got no strength."

"Pierre can run down to buy some food." Olivette spoke from behind Imamu.

"No, he can't," Imamu snapped. "This is my house. If anybody goes to the store, I will."

"It's cool, man," Pierre said, his large green eyes pleading. "That's my bag. I dig shopping. . . ."

Two things struck Imamu: The difference in the brothers' patterns of speaking, and the way Pierre's street talk contrasted with his gentle poetic face. He tried to listen with his inner ear to sense who was the phony, who was real. He would have bet on Pierre—but he didn't know.

"Get me some poke chops," Furgerson joked, smacking his lips. "I'll be the cook."

"No cooks, only painters," Imamu said. And to Pierre, "Get bread and sandwich meat. . . ."

"And Cokes and cake and milk—include hot dogs and ham with that meat. Hope you ain't got nothing against boiling a few franks just because it's your house, man . . ."

Imamu reached into his pocket, took out a ten-dollar bill, and handed it to Pierre.

"I'll take care of this," Olivette said, reaching toward his pocket.

"No way," Imamu said with a fierce pride. "If you want to help me paint, that's okay with me. But in this house, I do the feeding."

Olivette smiled. God, but the dude was handsome. Imamu's mind traveled through a dozen chambers wondering if he would let Gail meet the dude. Jealous? He had never been before. What was all that about?

"Where's your ladder?" Olivette asked with the same high-handed voice when Pierre had gone. Imamu moved his toothpick around with his lips and walked behind Olivette into the bedroom, where he stood in the doorway, fingertips in his back pockets.

"Ain't got none," he said after a few seconds.

"Doesn't your super have one?"

"In this house we call them janitors," Imamu said.

"Whatever—does he have a ladder?"

"Dunno." Imamu shrugged. "That cat ain't even got a wrench down there."

"Why don't I go down and ask?" Olivette said. "Did you say you had newspapers?"

"Why waste your time?" Imamu said. "Unless you want some sneaky pete. . . ."

"You don't have newspapers," Olivette said. "We'll collect some. Come with me, Furgerson. I'll need your help. . . ." And he walked down the hallway.

"All the way back down those steps—and back?" Furgerson said, but he followed.

Imamu looked after them feeling deserted. Olivette tried to pretend he wasn't there to waste time. Well, neither was he. He jumped to the dresser again, this time attacking the ceiling with energy. But with his first thrust a big clump of plaster broke off and fell on his head. Dust flew into his eyes. Imamu jumped down, wiped his eyes. But dust was on his hands. Feeling for the bed, once again he grabbed the sheet and wiped his eyes, then sat down on the bed, feeling helpless.

He sat until he heard voices approaching the door, then went to open it. Furgerson and Olivette

walked in with a ladder between them and newspapers
under their arms. "Your janitor didn't have canvas,"
Olivette said. "Newspapers will have to do. Spread it
around, will you, Imamu?" Imamu hesitated, wondering
if he would obey. Olivette looked at him, his eyebrows
raised. Then he laughed. "Look at you," he said. Going
to Imamu, he brushed plaster from his hair. Then taking
a sheet of newspaper, he folded it into a dunce cap and
put it on Imamu's head. "Bet that works better," he said.
Furgerson laughed. That pushed Imamu's anger up.

"What do you want me to do, Olivette?" Furgerson
asked.

"It seems we ought to decide what room we'll work on
first and move the furniture from it to give us more
space. Wouldn't you think so, Imamu?"

And because Imamu hadn't thought about it, hadn't
been about to think about it, and so had no right to be
angry with Furgerson for asking Olivette for direction, he
grunted.

"Right," Olivette said. "You and Pierre can start in
the back. Imamu and I can work the front. So why don't
we put the furniture in Imamu's room and the back of
the hall? That way you can start on the bathroom—after
lunch," he laughed, looking at Furgerson's face. "Imamu
and I can keep on with the bedroom—if that's all right
with you, Imamu?"

Imamu grunted.

"Good. Then we'll start moving the furniture and
spreading out newspapers—before we eat. All right,
Imamu . . . ?"

Imamu grunted.

Fighting resentment, Imamu looked on while Olivette
directed Furgerson where to spread the newspapers. Pi-

erre came in, wide eyes looking from Imamu to Olivette as though trying to measure how far they had gone—in anger? friendship? Strange kid. Sensing that Pierre would have preferred anger pulled him closer to the boy. He winked. Pierre grinned as he went to his brother to find out what was expected of him.

Furgerson and Pierre moved the dresser. While they were taking it down the hall, Olivette opened up the ladder. "Do you want to try it now, Imamu?" Imamu wanted to refuse, but realizing that that would be stupid, he climbed the ladder. It brought him much higher and to his amazement the scraping went much more quickly.

Smiling, Olivette looked up at him. "I believe in perfection," he said. "The best way to reach perfection is to make it as easy as possible to reach. Don't you agree?" He waited and when Imamu didn't answer went on. "We lived in this terrible old house in New Orleans. This gentleman friend of Mother's—a lovely man—decided it had to be painted. 'Painting is like everything else,' he used to say. 'It's all about learning the basics, and then reaching for perfection. . . .' We changed that old house into a palace. That old gentleman had quite an influence on me. . . ."

"Who gives a good godda—"

"Please." Olivette's sharp rebuke halted Imamu's rush of words. "We don't have to be abusive."

"I just said," Imamu said defensively, "that I don't care if this place don't look like no palace just so long as it's clean."

"But it's you who must live here."

"Yeah, until the damn thing caves in—I guess. And judging from the other buildings around . . ."

"Yes, these inner cities. Horrible. Their ugliness can

so easily creep into us. That's why when we work, when
we talk . . . we must sharpen the differences between us
. . . and them. . . ."

So, Olivette was the phony. Imamu could spot them a
mile off. He looked down at Olivette, and saw him un-
wrapping a bag he had brought in. He took out some
paint-brushes, a scraper, and an old shirt, which he put
on. Taking the scraper, he started on the opposite wall,
working silently, quickly. There was nothing for Imamu
to do but work on.

They had not spoken a word when Imamu heard Pierre going into the kitchen. Guessing that Furgerson had
sent him, he got down. By that time Olivette had finished
almost half the wall.

Going into the kitchen, Imamu found Pierre emptying
the bag of groceries. "Pierre," he said in a low voice.
"How old is your brother?"

"Eighteen," Pierre said, matching his near whisper.

"No jive—thought he was eighty."

"He'll be nineteen in December. . . . I'm fourteen.
Just got that way."

"No jive? So, you all come from New Orleans?"

"Born there," Pierre said. "But, man—we lived just
about everywhere. Detroit, Chicago, St. Louis. . . . We
just left East St. Louis. . . ."

"You dudes sure do move around. . . ."

"Yeah—but I dig this town," Pierre said. "Sure would
hate to leave it." His big dreamy eyes puzzled Imamu.
Such a contrast between the soft face and the down talk.

"Great block you live in," Imamu said. "Brownstone?"

"Yeah—one room with kitchenette. A damn sight better than the crum joint we padded down in in East St.

Louis. But I don't think my brother digs this town much."

"May I help?" Olivette's voice right behind them made them both jump.

"Man," Imamu said to Pierre, changing the subject. "What you got in this bag? You got to be a magician to make the bill I give you stretch to get all of this. . . ." Instead of sliced ham, Pierre had bought a canned ham. And along with everything asked for, he had brought paper plates, cups, napkins—and a box of toothpicks.

"How much did you give him?" Olivette asked.

"Twenty bucks," Pierre said quickly. And because of the fear lurking in the shadow of his eyes, Imamu didn't say he had given him only ten. Instead he growled at Olivette, who had opened up the loaf of bread, "Man, I can put meat between two slices of bread without help."

Calmly, Olivette went about setting the table. "Has your mother been ill long?" he asked.

"Why?" Imamu snapped.

"Oh? Isn't one supposed to ask?"

Most folks around the neighborhood knew about Imamu's mother. No one dared mention her condition to him. So putting on his worst street voice, he asked, "Your old lady sick, too . . . ?"

Olivette's deep golden eyes darkened with his I-like-you smile. "Mother? Heavens no. Mother's remarkably healthy—spoiled a bit. But so healthy. She's quite lovely." He kept smiling. "You'll meet her. You absolutely must. . . ."

Imamu bent his head over the sandwich he was making, wondering why there always seemed to be more to Olivette's words than he was saying. He kept silent,

knowing he was acting the fool, had been acting stupid
ever since the boy had walked into the house. Why? If he
accepted Olivette's help, he had also accepted his friendship. Yet he felt himself being commanded—being
pushed into a relationship whether he wanted it or not.
And he'd be damned. He chose the folks he wanted to be
with. And the folks whose mothers he wanted to meet.
He looked at Olivette to tell him so. Olivette smiled.
How could he look into that smile and be nasty? Before
he had a chance to say anything, Furgerson came stum-
bling into the room, gasping:

"Food, food, man. Feed me, feed me, 'fore I die—or
quit. . . ."

4

Under Olivette's direction the work went quickly. In three days the entire apartment had been scraped and Imamu's mother's bedroom painted. Olivette's energy was amazing. He drove them. His skill in mixing paint impressed Imamu. He insisted on mixing all the paint.

"Exciting isn't it?" Olivette said when Furgerson and Pierre had brought back the bed and put it in its place in the bedroom. Instead of agreeing, Imamu fumbled in his shirt for a toothpick.

But the old room looked like something he had never dreamed of. Done in shades of blue, with the bed moved against the darkest shade, it seemed to be in an alcove. The other walls had been painted dark, but then had been lightened with light blue and white paint from a sponge that gave it texture and camouflaged most of the ugly cracks.

"Just think," Olivette said, his cultured voice ringing with pleasure, "a bit of imagination and *voilà*, a hovel changes into a palace."

Irritated that Olivette never waited for praise, Imamu

heard himself answering. "Yeah—a li'l old paint sure can work miracles. . . ."

"And you chose the colors," Olivette said generously. Imamu flushed with guilt and embarrassment. He looked away from Olivette's giving smile.

"Man, you sure knows your stuff," Furgerson said. "If you'd just get here earlier in the mornings, we'd have been finished with the whole place. To have it look like this—wow."

"I'm not at my best painting until the sun moves nearer the west," Olivette said, and Imamu wondered why he didn't point out to Furgerson that he worked late nights, long after Furgerson had gone. Sometimes he worked until eight, even nine, o'clock. Did he have to act so generous? Imamu felt Pierre's eyes on him, and knowing the boy expected him to say something, to show up his brother's magnanimity for what it was, felt slightly stupid when all he could think of was: "You act like you been doing this kind of work a long time. . . ."

"We're inner city dwellers. Have been for a long time." Olivette spoke majestically. "We move around like gypsies, you know. . . ."

"And you dig that?" Imamu asked, wondering why that was something to be so proud about.

"Every place brings new understanding—new friends." Olivette's eyes included Imamu. And feeling Pierre's eyes begging him to be brilliant, Imamu tried again:

"And a new coat of paint. . . ."

"Exactly—a new commitment—to perfection. . . ."

How did Pierre expect him to top this word-throwing dude, Imamu thought as he saw Pierre turn away, disappointed. He had never heard anyone who liked to hear

himself talk so much—and what was worse, knew how
to. Olivette had more polish than anyone he had ever
heard—except maybe in old movies on TV. He had been
listening to him for days. Three days now. Three days!
Damn—Gail must have gone off to Jamaica. And he
hadn't called to say good-bye. Angry with himself, he
pried open a new can of paint, then taking a stick, began
to stir.

"By the way," Olivette said. "Where do you keep your
books?"

Pretending he hadn't heard, Imamu got up and stood
looking around for the place to start. Olivette followed
him and stood silently watching as Imamu looked
around the empty room.

"Books . . . ?" Imamu said as though he had just
heard. His face flamed.

"Yes," Olivette answered. "I've been looking around
to see what kind of literature you read. . . . I haven't
come across any. . . ."

"I do my reading in the library," Imamu said.

"Oh—I wondered." Olivette caught his eyes, register-
ing his doubt. "I found it strange not seeing . . . even a
magazine. . . ." He waited and when Imamu didn't answer went on: "I did expect to find something. You're
not like the others around here."

"How so?"

"There's a big difference—texturally." Obviously,
Olivette meant that as a compliment. Imamu's face
glowed with pleasure. Shyness misted his eyes. He
looked away. "This painting of the place is only an ex-
ample. I know only one other person who would do
something like it for his mother—me. . . ."

"Oh, you do feel an obligation to help your old lady?"

"Most of the boys our age around here seem to have gone beyond living. . . ."

"To junk," Imamu said. And Furgerson who had come to stand in the doorway added:

"We used to be a tough crowd around here, man. Times were when a new somebody came around this neighborhood, they had to fight to prove they were tough enough to stay. Now if they on junk, they come around to squat—a real frat, man. . . ."

"Things changed," Imamu said. "Guys moved away, got religion, or went on junk. I went to religion. I used to be a Muslim. . . ."

"That hardly accounts for the difference between you and the rest," Olivette said. "I have known many Muslims."

"That and other things." Imamu had been thinking of the Aimsleys, of Gail—the books they had read together, the discussing, the arguments.

"The brotherhood Imamu belonged to was made up of tough guys," Furgerson said. "That got all busted up— all on account of Imamu's boy, Iggy. He offed one old man, and the rest of them went in to deep religion or to jail—or else they dead. Muhammed, Imamu's good friend, got both jail and death. He got it right in the gut—on account of Imamu's boy. . . ."

"Come off it, Furgie," Imamu said. "You don't know that. They letting him out. . . ."

"Who cares what they do—or say. Don't nobody have to draw me no pictures—not if Muhammed got it in the gut after a phony confession."

"Even crazy studs can be innocent, Furgie."

"That's one stud who would be guilty even if he was

innocent. And they letting him out. I'll tell you one thing, when he heads for his best buddy, Imamu boy—you got a lot of painting to finish. . . ."

"You're not happy about your friend coming out?" Olivette asked, searching Imamu's face.

"He killed a man." Imamu spoke harshly to shock the smile from Olivette's eyes. "I was there. I saw him."

"What did you do?"

"Cut out. Ran and hid. . . ." Imamu remembered Iggy with the gun, the old man's white face getting whiter. He shuddered. "They caught me anyway. Iggy confessed to get me out."

"Then he is a good friend," Olivette said.

"He done it," Furgerson said. "That crazy mother-for-yer done it. Why shouldn't he confess?"

"If he confessed—I can't see why you two should count him out," Olivette said. "Didn't your religion teach the redemption of the soul . . . ?"

Furgerson did a double take, turned incredulous eyes on Imamu. "About time I got back to work," he said, waddling out.

Olivette went into the other room and started mixing paint. He worked in silence. And Imamu, standing behind him, studied his broad back, the strength of his arms beneath his knitted turtleneck. He wanted to ask if he played basketball, lifted weights. But knew if he did, he'd have to listen to that perfection routine again. "You seem to make it okay around here," he said finally. "The guys don't seem to bother you."

"Why should they?"

"Well, you look—dress—so cool—as though you ain't in a bad way. You're new, not on junk, yet the junkies never mess with you. . . ."

"I suppose it's because I'm not afraid of them. I don't mind standing around talking to them. . . ."

"Then why do you hate the neighborhood?"

"What is there to like about it? What is there to admire in junkies? One inner city, Imamu, is much the same as any other—ugly, destructive—of people, of families. . . . At any rate, it doesn't matter. Mother and Pierre are ready to settle down. I suppose here is just as good a place as any. . . . Mother has some strange hope that she might get me to go back to college. She has Fordham, Columbia in mind."

"Oh, a college kid . . . ?" The sneer in his voice surprised Imamu. He had nothing against college kids. Gail went to college and he dug her—the most. They often talked—joked—about him getting his equivalency and going. Maybe it was because Olivette talked about living in the "inner cities" like he was wearing a medal.

"No, not really," Olivette said. "School bores me. . . ."

"But you read a lot?" Imamu said. "Making it all the way to college ain't no small thing. . . ."

"I made it—in a matter of speaking. . . ."

"What manner is that?"

"I pass tests—quite highly—really. That compensates for my not being able to sit in classrooms."

"No jive?" Imamu's interest perked. If just reading could get you there. . . . He really looked at Olivette— his broad shoulders, his thick neck, the smooth, tan face. Olivette looked up with his I-like-you smile. Imamu found his eyes smiling back. "Four walls gives me a locked in feeling, too," he said. "Never been able to cut it. . . ."

"That's why I'm so surprised you have no books."

"What's books got to do with it?"

"Everything. How else does one pass tests . . . ?"

"What tests, man?"

Imamu tried to push up his resentment at the superior
edge in Olivette's tone. But a new feeling about the dude
prevented it. He had promised Gail to read more; he
hadn't. He had promised to check out summer schools.
He had flubbed out on that, too.

"Everything that can be taught in the front of a room,
Imamu, is written in books."

"Even math?"

"Even math—if the mind is good enough." He smiled
to indicate that most folks didn't have that kind of mind.
"It's all there. . . ."

"Man, you think that all you got to do is read and you
can pass tests—for Columbia. You living in a dream. . . ."

"But I have, Imamu. I have been to college. A seminary. I had thought to go into the priesthood. We're
Catholics, you know? I won a scholarship. . . . Mother
worked hard to get it, she managed to even meet the
cardinal—a lovely man. She managed to convince him
that despite my age—I really did know everything. My
mother—she has such winning ways. . . . And so I took
the test. . . ."

A priest? A goddamn priest—no wonder. No wonder. . . .

"You see, Mother had this gentleman friend—a gambler, I think. . . ." Olivette stopped to reflect. "Yes, quite
a fellow—lovely. He insisted on study. 'Involve yourself
as deeply as the mind allows in the printed pages of life,'
he used to say. 'Tolerate no interference with the work of
the mind and you shall achieve perfection. . . .' Great
mind. Great man. I can't tell you how deep an influence
he had on me. . . ."

"Wasn't he a painter?" Imamu retorted.

"No—no, this one was a gambler—excellent—never lost a hand. . . ."

Questions jumped to Imamu's mind. He fumbled in his pocket for a toothpick, which he stuck in his mouth, forcing himself to look away from Olivette. He felt Olivette's stare, boring into his head; he sensed the boy's disappointment that he hadn't given him the chance to explain. And Imamu felt pleased with himself.

Olivette waited for some time before he finally broke the silence. "I suppose you know how glad I am to meet you, Imamu. I do hope that you haven't thought me pushy—or that I was trying to interfere—anything like that. . . ."

"Now why would I think a thing like that?" Imamu asked, feeling on top of the situation for the first time since Olivette had walked into his house. "You must know you've been lots of help."

"Yes, I do. I like to see things done—well . . ."

"Sure, sure, you'd hate it if a feller didn't see what a wise guy you are. . . . Right?"

"No, I'm really no smarter than anyone, you know?" Olivette said, standing up to face him. "I just work so much harder trying. . . ."

And there, Imamu thought, is what comes from saying one sentence too many. He tried to look away from Olivette to discourage any further talk. But he couldn't. Olivette stood before him looking at him, forcing him to return the look. Their eyes met. Olivette kept smiling. "Okay," Imamu said, smiling too. "Okay—got the message. . . ."

5

Imamu had hoped that he and Furgerson would have moved the furniture out of his room so that they might start painting it when Olivette came the next day. But at ten-thirty Furgerson still hadn't come. He thought of going to his house to get him, but what if they missed each other on the way?

Another hot day. The crumbling buildings had given up their ghosts to the street. Crowds stood waiting for Stuff Smith—with or without his white boss. Kids running in and out of the bombed-out shells of buildings kept up a screaming laughter which rose to his window. So happy, so carefree, so unaware that they were being conditioned, in the squalor of their caves, to take over when this generation of ghosts passed on.

Imamu realized, suddenly, that he hadn't been outside for days. And having not been, he had no desire to leave the security of his walls, his locked door. No swagger, no pretense, no tensions. God! Sticking in the house would make him into an oldy—like the old men and old women of the neighborhood, who came out of doors only to make it to church, or to the post office to get their social security checks, get them cashed, buy groceries, then rush back to sit in front of TV sets, barricaded behind their doors—prisoners in their homes.

At the thought, Imamu headed for the door, without even changing from his paint-spattered clothes. Downstairs, he stood longer than necessary on the stoop, a toothpick in his mouth, forcing his eyes to a blank hardness. Slowly he started up the block. As he neared the corner, staring eyes forced him to turn. He saw the police car parked a few feet away with the two policemen looking at him. Imamu sloped his shoulders, and affecting a long stride and rolling gait, he crossed in front of the car, pretending they were not there. They knew him. With the precinct just around the corner, the dudes knew most of the cops and the cops knew them. Not having seen him for days, of course, they assumed he had been somewhere up to some kind of mischief.

Across the street Imamu called over the heads of the numbers players: "Hey, Al Stacy. . . ."

"Youngblood," Al Stacy called back. "Where you been hiding, man?"

"One guess," Imamu said, opening his arms for the gambler to look at his paint-splattered clothes.

"How's it going?"

"Beautiful, man. Won't be long now."

"Can I do you for anything?"

"You done enough. What I need more than most things is Furgerson. Seen him?"

"Naw. . . ."

"If he passes, give him a shout I'm in here. . . ." Imamu went into the pool hall to the telephone. As he dialed and stood listening to the ringing at the other end, he looked over at the patrol car and the policemen star-

ing across at the doorway of the pool hall. And it came
to him that around their end of town, they all were under
house arrest. Only when they stayed locked behind their
doors could they pretend that wasn't so.

"Hello, hello . . ."

"Mrs. Aimsley? Imamu . . ."

"Is anything wrong, Imamu?"

"No—called to find out if Gail got off okay."

"Yes. She was angry that you didn't call. . . ."

"Got stuck in the house—painting." That didn't sound
like a reason. Yet it had been the reason. So involved
with Mr. Perfection he had let the time slip by. "I—I
promised her I'd finish before she got back. . . . It's a
lot of work . . ." The reasoning sounded phony even to
his ears—but what else . . . ?

"Well I won't give you her *exact* message," Mrs.
Aimsley laughed. "But the way she left, I'd say she got
to Jamaica well ahead of her plane."

"Gosh, I'm sorry. I'll make it up to her. I'm working
day and night. . . ."

"Do you have help?"

"Sort of. . . ." He hesitated telling her about Olivette
—how accomplished, good-looking, interesting he was.
Still, if they remained friends, Gail had to meet him—
sometime. "The dude who's helping me out seems to
know what he's about. . . ."

"Too bad she can't reach you. . . . But she's only gone
for two weeks. Is there anything you need, Imamu?"

"No. . . ."

"Are you sure . . . ?"

"Sure. . . ."

"Will you promise to call if you need me . . . ?"

A wistfulness touched Imamu, thinking of his foster

mother's sweet, good-looking face—creased with anxiety and concern as she spoke to him. Mrs. Aimsley wanted him to need her—go to her. She had never forgiven herself for having turned on him, believing him responsible for her little daughter Perk's disappearance. He had stayed with Ann and Peter Aimsley only a few months— just enough time for Perk to have disappeared—and be found murdered. It had been a time for proving. A time for faith. A time for loving and forgiving. He had proved himself. Gail's faith and love had helped him do that. Forgiving? He had forgiven Mrs. Aimsley for the time of doubt. He even understood why she had. But her doubt, in the final analysis, had been important in his decision to leave the brownstone, and all that living with his foster family had come to mean. He loved Mrs. Aimsley. She had saved him. Not only from reform school. She had saved his mind at a time when it had been doomed to be forever trapped in the slumber of the slums. She had opened up a world where he had found new meaning.

"Okay . . . sure, I'll call—if I need you," he said to put her conscience at ease. Then seeing Furgerson skirting Al Stacy's group on his way to the corner, he said good-bye and hung up to rush outside.

"Hey, Furgie, where you been?" he called out to his friend.

Furgerson spun around, stood an undecided moment, staring at Imamu, then said, "I been to the unemploymnt office, man. . . . What's more, I got me a slave. I start tomorrow, early in the morning, you dig . . . ?"

"You got to be kidding. With all that we got left to do?"

"Painting? Man, you got nothing but help. But the

way I look at it, it just ain't safe around these streets—
no more."

"What happened? Got picked up again?" Imamu
looked across at the patrol car.

"Almost. But I seen the pigs stopping folks before
they seen me, when I left your pad last night. I hid in
your cellar."

Al Stacy had finished with his customers. He walked
over to join them. "What I been telling you?" he said.
"Whomsoever is pulling them jobs is making us trouble.
Messing with us, man. Messing with business. . . ."

"Al Stacy, you don't even know if it's one of our
boys," Imamu said.

"Don't know. And like I say, don't want to know—
'cause if the pigs squeeze me I might shout. You know I
don't go for folks messing with business. So I just wants
whomever to quit laying trails leading to here." He
pointed to the sidewalk.

"What trails, man?"

"Police ain't telling, but they mighty thick around. . . ."

"Don't see how that's messing with you, Al Stacy,"
Imamu said.

"Yet," Al Stacy answered. "But they been sniffing.
Now I can tell when a hound dog's sniffing—trying to
connect somebody with this here phantom—I sure hope
it ain't me. . . ."

Imamu stared at Al Stacy, thinking of the precinct on
the next block, and how the stud stood out there every
day, getting rich off the numbers. Then Furgerson said:

"And that ain't all, man. I seen Iggy. I seen them
pulling him in last night."

"Iggy! But he just got out!"

"They pulled him in just the same."

"But he can prove . . ."

"Which is more than the rest of us can. Which makes things hot around here. What? Iggy—and the police, too? He was heading right to you, man."

"Who—Iggy?"

"Yeah, that's who. Caught him right near your stoop. So—this morning, bright and early—I was the first on the employment line when they opened the door. . . . What is more—I got me a job. Delivery boy at a supermarket in Brooklyn. . . ."

"All the way in Brooklyn . . . ?"

"At the other end," Furgerson said. "And that ain't far enough. It take me two hours to get there and two hours back—sleeping and sweating all the way. Which means, Imamu boy, I won't be seeing you again—until fall. By that time, I guess Iggy will be gone in again. . . ."

"Just like that you running out on me?"

"With Iggy around, you won't be needing me—no more. . . ."

Imamu stood watching Furgerson walking up the avenue, his back twitching with the knowledge that he was being watched, and glad of it. Then he abruptly turned and pointed to the patrol car. "They pulled me in. They pulled Iggy in. You-are-next. Hurry with that paint job, my man. . . ." Then he crossed the avenue, turned the street, and walked out of sight.

Imamu swaggered back across the street, in front of the patrol car, jauntily. He ran up the stoop, went into his building but when he tried to walk up the stairs, his legs got weak. It took all his will to make his feet take him, step by step, to the top floor. When he opened the door, the smell of paint rushing at him made him wish he could change places with Furgerson. How much better to be working, to be able to stay away from the block from sunup to sundown.

Standing in the doorway of his bedroom, looking at the packed-in furniture, he thought of Gail. How many years of trying would it take to get to her? He had known and loved her just over a year, and still he dreamed of a happy ending. What the hell was a happy ending? Years stretched out before him, over him like an obstacle course. How many years would he live to see? Death was so much a part of the street scene. He was eighteen—would he make it to twenty-eight?

The doorbell rang. Imamu went to open it to Pierre and Olivette. "Look," he greeted them, "you guys been great. But I have had it. What sense is there in all of this . . . ?" He made a helpless gesture at his crowded bedroom, the hall. "What's it all about?"

Olivette looked at Imamu's face, studied it, then said: "Pierre and I will clear out this room."

"That's not my worry," Imamu said, feeling tears nearing the surface of his eyes. "Why should we—anybody—have to tire themselves with all this junk, in a place like this . . . ?" He gazed into the straight stare of Olivette. "To please a mother who couldn't care less," he said. "To show myself up as a good guy? To show you up as a great guy . . . ?"

A silence followed, a long silence. Then Pierre said: "Imamu, I'm not tired. I don't mind helping out. . . ."

"You see?" Olivette smiled. Imamu turned on Pierre.

"What in the hell do you mind doing?" he almost shouted. He hated suddenly that Pierre hung around waiting for Olivette to push him around, when beneath those green innocent eyes, resentment kept chasing resentment—at being pushed around.

Instead of answering, Pierre went into the room and began to pull on a mattress that leaned against the other furniture. "What do you want me to do, Olivette?" he asked. Imamu stared at Pierre. Was the kid retarded or something?

"I do feel so sorry for your friend," Olivette said, taking hold of the other end of the mattress. And for a moment Imamu sensed he was being manipulated in a dream.

"Furgerson?" Imamu asked.

"No, Iggy."

"What's Iggy got to do with anything?" Imamu's anger started rising.

"Isn't that what's upsetting you?" Olivette said. "I just saw Furgerson—he was telling me. . . . It must be terrible to come home—or wherever you call home—and have people running away because they're afraid."

"Maybe he deserves his reputation," Imamu said, looking at them struggling to get the mattress straight to take up the hall.

"No—not entirely, I'm sure. Poor boy. How is he supposed to act? What is he supposed to do, if he comes where he should have friends and he so clearly has no friends?"

Sweat jumped out on Imamu's neck. "I guess all that reading you be doing—going to that seminary and stuff —got you thinking you know folks pretty good?" he said.

"It really has," Olivette answered. They had come to the bedroom, and putting his end down, Olivette waited as Pierre went into the room to pull the front of the mattress in.

"Well, you don't," Imamu snapped.

"Oh, I don't know. . . ."

"Well, I do. There's lots of types you can't even begin to know."

"If I don't, it's not because of not trying," Olivette said. "Those whom I might never meet, I read up on."

"What am I supposed to say behind that?" Imamu said, sneering, aware of Pierre, standing in the middle of the room looking at him. "That you're some goddamn kind of brilliant dude—or God . . . ?"

Olivette turned to catch Imamu's eyes. "You're being abusive again."

"Who gives one good goddamn?" Imamu said.

"Do you really want me to leave?" Olivette's tan face had reddened. His shoulders had squared, his fists clenched and unclenched.

Imamu took the toothpick from his mouth, threw it on the floor, then heard himself say, "Sorry, man." Feeling a tinge of regret that he was letting down Pierre, maybe even letting himself down. But he was glad that his anger, their quarrel, had pushed aside his sadness, washed away his depression. Still, apologizing was a thing he did only in dreams.

He walked to his room and, grabbing the inner spring mattress, started up the hall to show he didn't need much help. He met Olivette coming back down, and looking in his eyes, said, "Being smart ain't nothing to apologize about. But you got to know one thing, man, you ain't no damn mind reader."

He had made up his mind that if Olivette repeated his threat to leave, he would open the door and show him

the way out. Olivette stared back. "Is that why you're
trying not to like me?" he asked. "Because you think I'm
able to read your mind?"

Olivette had hit near the truth. So instead of answering, Imamu tried to think of the harshest-sounding curse
words he knew. But after a few seconds, said, "My mind
ain't no open book, Olivette. You might think you're the
nearest thing to a preacher on Eighth Avenue, but there's
lots of minds around that it would take the Lord God,
Jesus Christ, to read . . . and with a lot of help."

"I was hoping you didn't," Olivette said.

"Didn't what, man?"

"Want me to leave, of course." Olivette looked as
deep into Imamu as eyes would allow. "I wouldn't have
wanted that. We've become so close. . . ."

Imamu didn't know whether the prickly heat bursting
from his back and from under his arms was caused by
anger or embarrassment. He stood glowering, forcing his
hands to keep from scratching, tongue-tied, fumbling for
an answer. Then the bell rang.

He leaned down the inner spring against the wall and
rushed to answer. But when he put his hand on the knob,
he snatched it away. Habit had suggested Furgerson. But
of course it wasn't. Iggy? He wanted to turn away, but
sensed Olivette, waiting. He opened the door.

Gladys stood there in the hall, breezy-looking in a see-
through print dress that revealed her braless top and the
lines where her panties began and ended. She pushed
past Imamu into the hallway. "So this is where you got
him hid, Imamu Jones?" she said, going up to Olivette.
"What you doing with this pretty man tied up in here?
Baby . . ." She smiled up at Olivette. "I come to cut you
loose. . . ."

Grinning with relief that it hadn't been Iggy, Imamu said, "Hey, girl. . . ." And to Olivette, "Gladys—she's an old friend."

"I ain't old," Gladys snapped. "I'm real young, real pretty, and damn available."

"Long-time friend," Imamu said. "Been around since she was this high. . . ." He measured a meaningless distance.

"Don't need no introduction," Gladys said. "Your name is Olivette. I see you walking by my bed." She winked mischievously. "Bed's right by the window—so I really sees you. I been wanting to get next to you. Handsome dudes don't move into the neighborhood no more, and this clown's got the nerve to have you stashed. . . ."

Imamu kept grinning at Olivette's awkwardness. He had never spoken to Olivette about girls. Hadn't had the time. But in his mind he formed a picture of Gladys and Olivette together, with Olivette's hands traveling over her shapely, plump body, and of her suddenly opening up her garbage mouth. The thought had no sooner formed when Gladys said, "Yeah—been seeing you and that brother of yours." She indicated Pierre, farther down the hall, with a nod. "And sometimes when that red-headed wench. . . ."

Olivette's polite smile faded, a nerve twitched in his temple. "You're talking about Mother. . . ." he said.

"Oh, that who she is?" Gladys spoke without remorse. "Been wondering. Honey, I was ready to go through a mess of redheads to get to you. Bet you never guessed, when you walk down the block, that a real foxy chick got her eyes on you."

"Lay off my workmen, girl." Imamu joked to put Oli-

vette at his ease. "I pays them to use elbow grease not to
go through jive sessions."

"Damn, Imamu," Gladys answered. "Just because you
locked into that Brooklyn heifer, don't mean nobody else
wants this fine brown frame."

Imamu grabbed Gladys by her arm. If Olivette had to
leave because of sloppy talk, he'd just as soon it be his,
not Gladys's. "Come on, girl," he said. "I was on my
way to the store. Need somebody to help me buy grits to
keep my folks on the job." Gladys tried to pull away, but
Imamu kept his grip firm. "Ain't it time for you to go to
your slave, girl?"

"No, it ain't," Gladys said. "I work from six to twelve.
I ain't got nothing but some time." But his hand on her
arm gave her the message that, whatever her time, she
wasn't spending it there.

Peeved, as they walked up the avenue toward the supermarket, Gladys remained silent, but after a time she
said, "What's with that turkey anyhow? He don't seem
none too friendly."

"Give him time, baby. You're a lot of woman for a
dude like him to take all at once."

"Time. He ain't here in this neighborhood, with all
these junkies and stuff, because he's so damn innocent.
Don't matter if he got them sad eyes and sweet face."

Imamu wanted to add, And that holier-than-all-folks
attitude that drives me up the wall. Instead he said,
"Maybe the dude ain't your speed."

"What's that supposed to mean?" Gladys stopped
walking and turned to face him, her hands on her hips.
"What comes over you cats that gets close to a girl, then
pushes her off the minute a strange face shows up?"

"Strange face? It ain't that, Gladys. But guys grow up.

. . ." He wanted to add that a tough, ready type, no matter how cute with wet curls, probably wouldn't get near to an Olivette. "Girl, Olivette is a strange dude. He won't get close enough to smell that sewage you sling, 'less you wash your mouth out with lye. Even then you got to give him space. . . ."

He hooked her arm dragging her along, then slackened his hold as someone yelled, "Youngblood, let go my girl, there. . . ."

"Gotcha man," Imamu called back to Al Stacy, who had stopped his Cadillac to speak to them.

"What I tell you 'bout coming out on the avenue in them see-through things, gal," Al Stacy joked. "Don't want to have to go up side some simple sucker's head on your account. . . ."

"I can take care of myself," Gladys called back. When Al Stacy drove off, she said, "Taking care of this body is the thing I do best."

They had neared the market. Imamu stopped to say good-bye when he saw the police car, slowing down. So he kept holding on to Gladys's arm. "Al's got a real hard-on for you, girl," he said. "What's more, he got loot. . . ."

Imamu had no intention of going into the market then coming out to find cops outside waiting. Nor did he intend Gladys to leave until they had gone by. Witness. He always had to have witnesses. To breathe he had to have a witness—or they could haul him in and accuse him of not breathing. Keep him too, never let him out—who was around to protest? His mother? The Aimsleys? They were all the way in Brooklyn.

The patrol car drove by. Imamu said, "Bet you two end up getting married."

"I'm still too young to be taking charity," Gladys said.

"Charity like that beats begging."

"Man, I ain't started begging dudes—yet. . . ."

"Imamu, my man . . ." Imamu was about to let Gladys's arm go. The familiar voice made him grip it even tighter.

He waited until the wave of fear subsided; then putting a smile on, he turned. "Hey—Iggy. Whatcha know, man? Heard that maybe you'd be out."

Yes, there he stood, like out of a bad dream. He looked the same. No, not exactly. Iggy's face was still narrow, the beady eyes still crossed, the floppy cap he wore turned backward, covered part—but not all—of his inverted forehead. His grinning mouth revealed pointed teeth. But Iggy had grown! He had grown almost to Imamu's chin—in jail! Bets had been that Iggy would be a midget.

"Man," Iggy said. "I been in and out, then in again. No sooner I hit the street—yesterday—them bulls had me roped in, trying to get me on a shit-rap. Some slick mother-for-yer out here been giving them some hard times. They wanted it to be me. Would have made life easy for the jokers."

Imamu kept stretching his face into a smile. Seeing Iggy face to face was even harder than he had imagined. What to say? What to talk about? He actually hated the cat! He hated that he hated him. Because if Iggy hadn't changed, he loved Imamu. Had loved him since he was a kid. . . .

"Man," Iggy said. "Sure am glad to see you—and Gladys. Whatcha know, girl?" Iggy's eyes moved over Gladys, stopping to rest on her heavy breasts, before traveling down to her plump legs.

And Imamu remembered, suddenly, Iggy never had
had a girl. What things had he been thinking of locked
up with nothing but dirty talk and wet dreams? "Woman." Iggy kept showing his pointed, ratty-looking teeth.
"You sure looks good. What say we take a walk—and
do a li'l talking."

"Since when I been taking walks with you, you simple mother-for-yer?" Gladys's eyes flashed over Iggy, her
lips turning up to give her words an authentic twist. "The
only place I'd walk with you is up to the gates of hell—
to kick you the hell on in."

"That ain't no way to be talking to me. . . ."

"The way I wants to, is the way I talks, pressed head.
Yeah . . ." she said, as Iggy's hand reached to his back
pocket. "Just make sure what you comes out with, you
use it—or you gonna eat it."

"Hold it, hold it, man." Imamu reached an arm
around Iggy to restrain him. And there he was, starting
all over again. The same gestures, the same words. He
had done it before. It had been the biggest part of his
childhood. But now he wanted no part of it. No more!
What to do? What did one do when patience was worn,
when all sympathy had gone?

A patrol car drove by and Imamu looked his anger at
it, at the cops, the lawyers, judges, those educated dudes,
who had folks like him, like Furgerson, jumping through
loops, and couldn't keep a handle on the ones like Iggy.

"That's right," Iggy said, sneering. "Gladys always
been yours. Better make her hold her mouth or I'm
subject to forget. . . ."

Keeping his arm over Iggy's shoulders, Imamu guided
him away, leaving Gladys standing, hands on hips, blazing the avenue with her anger. "Don't take that simple

mother's-child nowhere," she said. "Let him stay and
mess up. He's living in a fist-sucking dream. I'm gonna
wake him. . . ."

Imamu felt Iggy's resistance under his arm and realized, with a chill, that this was new. Al Stacy had said
Iggy needed to be in the nuthouse. But here he was
breathing the same air that preserved them all—and the
Lord preserve them all. They crossed the avenue, and as
they stepped up onto the curb, Imamu heard:

"Iggy . . . ? You're Iggy. . . ." He had not seen Olivette on the corner waiting for them. But suddenly there
he was, the beatific smile lighting his clear face. His
warm eyes searched through Iggy's. "I am glad you're
out," he said, sticking out his hand. Iggy reached for his
back pocket. Olivette pretended not to see. "It must have
been terrible for you, being locked away from your
family—and friends—so long."

Iggy glanced at Imamu suspiciously. Slowly he moved
his hand from his pocket. But before it fell to his side,
Olivette had caught and covered it with both of his. Like
a bird, trapped, Iggy's beady eyes shifted from Olivette
to Imamu, and back.

Taking a toothpick, Imamu picked his teeth, trying
not to look at Olivette making like a priest. The dude
might have read every book ever written—even the well-
known stack of Bibles. He might have known every inner
city in the entire United States, but it was sure he had to
die and be reborn with a halo to know what was being
put down around the streets of this most inner city.

6

"Thought you had done forgot about me, son," she said, before he went up to the bed.

"Mama." He bent to kiss her, brushing back her soft, gray hair from her lined forehead, remembering for one painful moment when it hadn't been lined, but smooth, black, and shining. "Only way I'm about to do that is to be dead—and lady, that ain't about to happen—so long as you're here needing me."

Guilt made him hide his face as he got busy taking the bag of fruit he had brought out of the shopping bag with the cans of paint he'd bought on the way to the hospital. He put the fruit on the bed table. Even his best excuse— that he had been painting the apartment for her—didn't justify her being abandoned. But he hadn't even done much painting in the last few days—not since Iggy appeared around the block. Imamu spent most of the time now looking out of his window, waiting for Olivette. But Olivette was spending more and more time with Iggy. He was serious about rehabilitating Iggy.

"Now, don't you sound like a true gent'man," Mrs. Jones said, a faded smile fleeting across her face. That

effort forced him to remember back to when she had
been the pretty, great lady Al Stacy talked about. Her
eyes had been a gentle brown instead of a faded gray, her
hair had been black, her shining skin had gone with her
velvet ways. How long ago? A hundred years . . . ?

Sitting beside her bed, Imamu reached for her thin,
shaking hands and held them, thinking of the pain they
had shared: the death of his father in Vietnam; Imamu's
constant trips in and out—first on petty charges, then
bigger, bigger—until the charge had been murder (had
she actually believed him guilty? he refused to believe
that); his conversion to a religion completely alien to her
do-or-die Baptist faith; and then her battle with the rotgut sneaky pete. A lot for one woman to stand up under.

"Got yourself a job?" she asked.

"Naw . . ." And as fear slipped into the faded eyes, he
rushed to reassure her. "Been busy though—fixing up a
big surprise—for you. . . ."

"Reckon that can happen—again . . . ?" She examined
her pale fingers in hopelessness. "Last surprise was waking up in here to find I was still living. . . ."

But she had shown concern about his not finding
work. A good sign. Before, she had only shown concern
about where to get the next bottle. "Just you wait. . . ."
he said. "Wait until you get home. . . ."

"Home . . . ?" She pleated her brow, as though trying
to remember. Imamu silently let his mind lead hers from
the hospital to the subway, up the main street, onto the
avenue—their block—step by step past the nodding addicts, past the winos huddled together sharing space and
booze—waiting for her to come back . . . ? And his mind
refused to climb the stoop, to go up the stairs to the
apartment being so artistically painted.

Why hadn't he finished? What had been his excuse? Certainly not that Olivette had taken time off to fiddle around with Iggy's "potential."

"You wouldn't know the old place," he said, almost giving up the secret he had vowed to keep. Then thinking of her concern about his not working, added: "Everything will be cool, Mama—I'll have me a job, by the time we get you home. . . ."

She shook her head. "John," she said. She had never called him Imamu. "They was some good people—them fosters. . . . You should have stayed with them. . . ."

"They were okay," Imamu said, offhandedly, thinking of the anguish he had suffered when he had decided to leave the Aimsleys. He had not known that he had loved pretty houses, or quiet tree-lined streets. But he had made his choice. "Home is with you, Mama. It always was—always will be."

But why hadn't they cleaned up the addicts on his block—even those who sat nodding on the steps of the precinct? Why hadn't they jailed the pushers, put the dealers out of business? Made the streets clean! Why didn't the police catch their burglar instead of riding Imamu Jones's back! And suddenly Imamu admitted to the pressure on him, every time he walked the streets, to keep from being picked up, while his mother lay in the hospital—with no one around but him to care.

And his tension grew worse as he rode back uptown on the subway. Just the thought of walking the street with his shopping bag of paint, giving false ideas to the all-seeing addicts; of trying to keep invisible from the police, to get into his building, into his apartment, locking anxiety on the other side of this door—it was a goddamn circus tightrope act. . . .

Later, going through the turnstile at his stop, Imamu took a toothpick out of his pocket and put it into his mouth. Then climbing the steps, his heavy shopping bag hitting against his legs, he pushed past someone who seemed intent on blocking his way and stepped out into the hot street, stopping just long enough to change his long-legged hopping gait into a jaunty swagger.

"Imamu!" He turned.

"Olivette!" He cried, startled. Pleased. "What are you doing here?"

"Waiting for you. Don't you ever look at the poor people you push out of your way?"

"How did you know I'd be on the train . . . ?"

"You went to the hospital. I found out visiting hours, timed the trains—and *voilà*. . . . I've been waiting the better part of an hour," he admitted.

"How'd you know I went to the hospital?" Imamu asked.

"You weren't home. I looked around the block—no one had seen you. Two places you would go. To look for a job. The hospital. I took a chance that conscience and dedication must dictate." Olivette laughed affectionately. They fell into step, going up the block. "How are you getting on?" he asked.

"With the apartment?" Imamu asked, his eyes scanning the block as they walked. "Not so hot. . . . Sort of lost the urge—know what I mean?"

"Are you ready to work at it now?"

The question, What about Iggy? jumped to Imamu's mind. But he brushed it aside, knowing he would sound jealous, and asked, "Right now? Why not?"

They were nearing the group of buildings the church

had rehabilitated for senior citizens. And Imamu wanted to stop, to talk about how wonderful they looked with their big lighted stoops, the wide windows, and wonder aloud to Olivette about why more of the same couldn't happen all over for all the old folks—if not for every-body. But he never did because he spotted a patrol car cruising past, then slowing down as the policemen caught sight of them. His back tightened, and he twisted the toothpick at the side of his mouth. "Where is Pierre?" he asked.

"Pierre went to the movies with Iggy," Olivette said, and Imamu broke the toothpick by biting down too hard. No one, but no one, would get him to actually talk against Iggy. But Olivette ought to know an innocent like Pierre just didn't hang around with a way-out stud, after Imamu told him he'd committed murder. "I wanted Iggy to wait around for you. I thought he might like helping out."

"Helping out in what?"

"The apartment."

"Iggy? What you got in your head for brains, man?"

"Might do him good."

"What? Painting . . . ?"

"No—being with us—seeing us—the way we work together. . . ."

Imamu reached for another toothpick, his eyes on the patrol car. He felt the muscles on his neck tighten.

"What terrible crimes have been committed against him."

"Who?" Imamu turned to Olivette, pretending to look at him, but seeing only the car cruising by. They had come to a playground. He looked through the fence at the boys shooting baskets, keeping the cruising car in sight.

"Iggy," Olivette answered. He stopped beside Imamu and was looking in at the players. "Do you know that once his mother actually went to court and asked the judge to put Iggy away? He had run away from home. He was only nine."

"She had a tough time with Iggy." Imamu defended the woman he had always blamed.

"Iggy's spent most of his life locked away. . . ."

"Man, she ain't done all them things that landed the dude in jail. . . ."

"No. She's just as much victim, I suppose."

The policemen had parked the car and had got out. Adjusting their broad shoulders, their hands on their bulging holsters, they headed toward them. Holding tight to the shopping bag, Imamu ran.

Stop fool, stop. You ain't done nothing. Not guilty. Not guilty. Not guilty. He flew.

Feet pounded the sidewalk behind him. He ran up the block, turned the corner, ran down that block, turned another corner, ran across streets, zigzagging up one, down one, up one, down one.

His tensions were released by running. He felt light-headed. A recklessness came over him. Catch me, catch me, catch me, but don't touch me. Kill me, kill me, kill me, but don't hold me. Try, baby, try, try, try. . . .

And indeed, the world opened up to him, the sun sucked him upward, tunneled a path for his feet. He soared through space. The wind played music in his ears, gladdening him. Warm breezes slid over him like silk. How sweet a triumph. He laughed. Free. Free from blight, from people, up here rushing through the gold of a day, the air—clouds beneath his feet—the world, wide and empty, his alone.

With a shock the earth hit the bottom of his feet, knocking the air out of his lungs. He gasped, tried to coax the air back, to pull at the sun, to save the cushioning softness of the clouds, the support of the wind. He kept panting, his body bent, holding onto a stoop, for support. He looked around. He was far away from home —on the other side of City College.

"Imamu—Imamu. . . ." Olivette came running up to him. He too was panting, sweat from his brow, running down his cheeks, into a point at his chin—dripping. They looked at each other, panting. Leaning against the stoop, until the return of their strength, they walked down the hill, to St. Nicholas Park. Entering, they began crossing the park, horizontally, until they came to a boulder, midway, overlooking the street they had just run from. Throwing themselves to the ground, they waited for the return of their normal breathing, before Imamu said:

"Think we lost 'em?" He searched the streets below for police cars.

"Why did you run?" Olivette asked.

"Don't know. Just seen them suckers coming. Man, the feet took off like they was doing my thinking."

"Did you do something?"

"No—but them cats don't be caring about a li'l thing like that."

"So—what do we do now?" Olivette asked. "Just sit here until dark?"

Imamu realized that somewhere back there, he had dropped the paint. Gut reaction: Drop the goods and make it. Just keep out of the hands of the law. There had to be a better life. Where? There had never been for him—not really. Or for any of the guys he had come up with. . . .

Stretching out on the hard earth, and using a tuft of grass as a pillow, Imamu gazed up at the college looming over the park—handsome, remote—somebody's dream. He looked at Olivette lying next to him, leaning up on his elbow searching the street.

Had Olivette experienced what he, Imamu, had experienced? The thrill of the chase? The lightness of freedom? Had he given himself over to the wind? Had he felt the joy of being suspended between earth and sky?

"Why did you run?" Imamu asked, in turn.

"I saw you take off—so I ran along. . . ." Olivette smiled a we-shared-it smile. "Whatever happens to one —that sort of thing, you know?"

And there it was again—the feeling of the world opening up to him, of being a part of a golden day. And in the park where no flowers grew, where the gray boulders, the rocks, the earth which sprouted only an occasional tuft of grass here, weeds there, to remind one of once-upon-a-time and where trees dropped as much from sucking no substance from the unnourished earth as from the heat— the leaves brightened, skimpy branches fluttered into fullness and the greenness that brought together the rich, brown earth and the bluest sky, caught the shaft of sunlight that came pouring through them like gold. The surge of gladness within him, Imamu knew, came from having so brilliant a boy to care and show his caring, and having a friend for whom he cared, and to whom he wanted to show his caring.

"I went to meet his mother, you know. . . ." Olivette was saying. Imamu was barely listening.

"Who? What?"

"Iggy's mother," Olivette said. "She doesn't seem to like him. I believe she's disappointed that he's back home . . ."

Imamu kept trying to hold on to the glitter and warmth he had been experiencing. But suddenly the large leaves seemed to wither on their skimpy branches, the pebbly earth he had stretched out on became painful, the gold through the trees grew brassy, the sun hot and blinding. Feeling cross, he wondered how long they would have to wait there and if waiting really mattered. "No," he heard himself say. "Nobody likes Iggy—not even his old lady."

"Aren't you glad we befriended him?" Olivette said, looking down at Imamu, his golden-brown eyes serious, searching. Imamu avoided looking back. "How can anyone find the good in Iggy, Imamu, if no one is willing to search?"

"Maybe there ain't no good to be found," Imamu said

slowly. "Or maybe finding it is like searching for gold that a rattlesnake is guarding."

"But you're his friend," Olivette said. "At least Iggy seems to think so."

Imamu sat up. He plucked a blade of grass, which he put into his mouth. A difficult question. Was he a friend of Iggy's? Had he ever been? Could he ever be? He had never wished the dude harm. Never wanted to hurt him. But with the murder, he had had it with him. He didn't want Iggy around—wished he would never be in the neighborhood, around any block where he was—but that had never been his decision to make.

"I know the dude, Olivette," Imamu said. "I seen him slash open a cat, a dog—just for fun. He's always been that way. . . ." Imamu took a deep breath, thinking too of Iggy's confession that set Imamu free. "Some folks starts off with their brains scrambled. I'd keep Pierre away from him, Olivette."

"Pierre likes him," Olivette said. "They get along very well. Had you thought, Imamu, that that's what Iggy needs—someone to love him."

"Maybe," Imamu replied doubtfully. "But Olivette, I'd take it easy all the same—until you guys know your way around here. . . . Oh, I know"—Imamu waved Olivette's protest away—"you been living in worse places than this."

"They are all the same," Olivette answered. "In New York the buildings are taller, the streets more crowded—but a slum is a slum, Imamu. Poverty is the destroyer. . . ." He shuddered.

"Poverty, Imamu, can turn friend against friend, mother against children—children against parents. When that happens, children can talk loud, act bad—but whatever the reaction, they are alone. And when they're alone, inside—anything, or everything, happens.

"I'll always remember Brother Joseph—a fallen Jesuit. A friend of Mother's. . . . Oh, a lovely man. He came to me, after I had had an illness—in New Orleans. 'Poverty,' he used to say, 'is a crime against man, caused by men, because men are still basically savages. But if the modern world is to be saved,' he said, 'man must attempt to find a new way—a perfect way. . . .' Oh, he had a great influence on me. . . ."

"Then why did you drop out of the seminary?" Imamu asked.

"For the same reason Brother Joseph did," Olivette said. "I had read too much by the time I went in, I suppose. I had already read Gautama, Confucius, the life of Christ. . . . I had gone through Voltaire. And I knew that what I was being taught was not truth but conformity. . . . Have you ever studied history, Imamu?"

Looking down the street, Imamu saw a crowd gathering on Al Stacy's corner. He kept his eyes on them. "Who—me? Sure. . . ." he lied.

"Did you know that the Aborigines. . . ."

"The who?"

"Ab— American Indians. . . ."

"Oh. . . ."

"They worshiped the sun. . . ."

"Man, everybody knows that kind of history. They wasn't nothing but savages. They ain't known no better."

"Better?" Olivette's eyes searched Imamu's face. Imamu kept his eyes on the steadily growing crowd at the corner. "I have heard it said, Imamu, that whites took over this country because there was nobody here when they came."

"Now, I know that's a lie," Imamu said, pulling his eyes away to look at Olivette. "What about them Indians fighting cowboys? They got them on reservations."

"Exactly," Olivette said as though he had scored a victory.

"Them white folks was greedy, man. They said that to give them excuses to steal the land."

"But the country is populated by people who justify the killing and stealing *because* the Indians believed in the sun."

"No, I don't go for that," Imamu said. "We all know they didn't know about God. They never was taught. They were savages. . . ."

"Savages, Imamu? Can you think of anything that is possible without the sun?"

Imamu felt his back bristle. Sweat jumped out again on his cooling brow. He threw down the blade of grass and plucked another. "Well, ain't but one God, Olivette. And I guess He makes the sun do most things."

"Ahh, but how well the sun was doing most things for the Indians—until the white man brought their gods along. . . ."

Imamu stood up. The crowd on Al Stacy's corner was too big for the time of day.

As he walked down the hill, Olivette alongside, anxiety stirred in his chest. They climbed over the iron rail at the foot of the hill and walked toward the crowded corner, slowly, as though knowing that something threatening to them might be happening. They skirted the edge of the gathering people, and Imamu heard Gladys's voice.

"Let that fool come. Let him come," she cried. "Just let that dirty-mother-for-yer nose-picking turd come. . . ."

Imamu pushed through the crowd, until he found himself standing behind Iggy. Iggy had his switchblade out, waving the six inches of it at Al Stacy's stomach. Behind Al Stacy, being held back by his arm, Gladys Dawson stood, the upper part of her dress torn down to her waist, her full bosom exposed.

"Let me at that bitch," Iggy kept saying. "Let me at her. I ain't got nothing with you, Al Stacy—but if you don't move out of my way. . . ."

"For the last time, fool," Al Stacy said in a steady voice, his eyes narrowed on Iggy's face. "Don't make me do nothing against you. Don't be acting crazy on this corner, man. I don't want to hurt you. . . ."

No one had ever seen Al Stacy fight. No one had ever seen him with a piece. Still, folks didn't mess with Al Stacy. His reputation didn't stand for that. But seeing him trying to be cool, not one inch away from the moving blade had everyone paralyzed. One little plunge and Al Stacy wouldn't have time to say his last prayer.

"One second, man," Iggy threatened. "One second and you got it. . . ." He waited for what seemed minutes but was only a well-calculated second. Then he lunged. Al Stacy jumped back, put out his hand, and suddenly a twenty-two was in it, aimed at Iggy.

Imamu came up behind Iggy and laid an arm around his shoulders. "Man, you don't want to be messing up. You just got out. . . ."

Iggy tried to shrug Imamu's hand off. "I want that whore," he said. "She can't stay behind there all night."

"Come and get me. . . ." Gladys screeched from behind Al Stacy's protecting back. "Let the mother's child come. . . ."

"Iggy." Olivette moved to stand in front of Iggy, right

at the point of the knife. "Let's go. We have other things
—more important things. . . ."

The blade rested lightly on Olivette's chest. "Come on.
. . ." Olivette insisted, and Iggy looked up into his face.
He looked over at Gladys who was still straining to get at
him.

"Bitch—I'm gonna get you," he promised. Then with
a movement of his hand he sheathed the blade and pushed
the knife into his back pocket. Imamu felt his knees
buckle as Olivette pushed Iggy through the crowd.

"Man." Pierre spoke from behind Imamu as they
crossed the street. "Been looking all over for you dudes."

Surprised, Imamu looked at Pierre, and as they clus-
tered together on the opposite corner, he asked, "Where
did you look for us?"

Pierre's eyes stretched into their full roundness, which
seemed to take over his entire face. He glanced at his
brother, then back to Imamu. . . . "Up to your place," he
said quietly. Imamu looked away across the street where
Al Stacy was leading Gladys to his car, his coat around
her shoulders. She was still crying, cursing, threatening.

"Exactly what happened?" Imamu asked Pierre.

"We just come from the movie and was walking up the
block," Pierre explained. "Then we seen Gladys. Iggy
followed her. He kept talking and the chick wouldn't
answer. Then he grabbed her. . . ."

Stupid thing to do on Al Stacy's corner, Imamu
thought. "She socked him and called him some dirty
mothers—you know what. . . . So he went for her."

"Uh-huh . . ." Imamu murmured thoughtfully. Something was off in Pierre's explanation—a matter of timing.
But why?

"Iggy, I know you had no intention of doing Gladys

any real harm," Imamu heard Olivette say, his voice gentle. "She's Imamu's friend."

"I know her too, man," Iggy said, his voice insinuating. "I known her when."

Imamu tried to look away from the lie in Iggy's face. Then remembering what Olivette had said about Iggy's being unloved, he studied the tight, closed face, the blinking eyes, the tight mouth. It had to be tough without one person caring, that was sure. It was also tough to be bad and think that sex was the worst thing a stud had the *right* to enjoy. That made a bad, unloved stud dangerous. Iggy qualified. It would take more than Olivette's priest act to change that.

"You mustn't forget what I tell you," Olivette said. "If you want friends, the first thing you must learn to do is hold your temper." Olivette, fatherly. Cool. "Everyone reaches out to someone who tries . . ." Imamu twisted his lips around his toothpick, waiting for that overused word: perfection. But even Olivette knew better than to hit Iggy with that one. ". . . for gentleness," he said, laying his soft smile on Iggy's bent head as though it was a hand. "Even Gladys would—"

"Who cares what Gladys wants?" Iggy broke in. "She messed with me—and she's gonna pay."

"What did I tell you of always think—"

"Look, man, I hear you talking," Iggy said. "I been sitting around listening to all your bull, but I got to do something, see. . . ." He moved his tense body, restlessly, took out his switchblade, made some stabbing movements in the air.

"Like what, Iggy?" Olivette asked, quietly. "Like mugging some little old lady for her little bit of money?"

"Better than sitting around, listening to all that talk,

talk, talk—and about how to grow gentle. I got my ways. . . ."

"Iggy—you must give yourself a chance," Olivette said. Iggy put away his blade, looked around at them.

"I hear what you saying, man," he surprised Imamu by saying. "But I can't just hold still for it. While I'd be doing all this thinking and figuring you talking about— things be happening, man. . . ."

"It will do you good to come to Imamu's and help us," Olivette suggested.

"With what? Painting? No, man. Got to be something weirder than that. Painting? I got to do something for bread, man—lots of bread. . . ."

Olivette's mentioning paint forced Imamu to remember his flight and that he had lost the paint, which meant he had to wait for tomorrow—when his mother's check came—to buy more.

"Iggy, come on," Olivette said, with a touch of impatience. "Those old women you're likely to hit probably have much less than you do."

"Tough," Iggy said, moving about still restless, his eyes on Pierre. "You and them big words—and all that preaching. . . . Hell, I got to have action. . . . Come on, man," he said to Pierre, walking away. And Pierre took off behind him and fell in step with him.

Now what had Olivette thought he had accomplished with that little talk? Did he think he had blown air into Iggy's brain, opened up the corridors of his thoughts to oxygen? "Don't tell me you got after Iggy with that perfection thing?" Imamu asked.

"It would be good if he thinks about it."

"What good's thinking gonna do?"

"There's an area in most of us that wants to achieve

more. If Iggy doesn't know it's possible, how can you expect him to try?"

"It ain't possible for Iggy," Imamu insisted.

"Then you would leave him absolutely alone? That would be your solution?"

A damn good question, Imamu agreed. What did one do with an Iggy? Putting him in a foster home would destroy the home. Leaving him in the neighborhood imprisoned it even more, heightened the feeling of hopelessness, stilled even the loud laughter, the flashes of happiness.

"Olivette, I don't have solutions. I just know what will and what won't work."

"Do you feel that way about your mother?" Olivette asked, facing him. Imamu stilled the urge to tell him off, let him know he didn't play that. Leave his mother out of it. But the warmth they had shared in the park prevented him. The silence grew between them before Imamu finally asked:

"What way, man?"

"That nothing can be done about her alcoholism?"

"That's different."

"Is it? Why do you think she became alcoholic?"

"She used to be happy," Imamu said. "Then my old man died. . . . She ain't been the same since. . . ."

"And you blame her illness on his death—of course."

"They dug each other—the most," Imamu answered.

"And you think that you might be helping her, by painting the apartment and bringing her into it?"

"Something like that. . . ."

"But you know that alcoholism is an illness," Olivette said.

"Yes, I know," Imamu answered. "Some folks drink

all of their lives and never become alcoholics, others . . .
But if anything can be done to change her—then making
life better around her would be the thing."

"So, the house will look lovely—no doubt. But what if
your mother decides on that first drink? What if she
insists on it . . .?"

"She won't," Imamu said, pretending not to see the
winos—his mother's chums—as they walked onto the
block. How did he stop his mother from greeting them?
From accepting their hospitality? "She never got took to
the hospital in a coma before. So she'll think twice. . . ."

"Do you truly see it that way?"

"That's the way it is, man."

"You know you're deceiving yourself . . . ?"

"What the fu—" He bit the word back, even before he
felt the tightening of Olivette's body. He looked now to
see the muscle twitch in his face. God, the perfection
required to be this turkey's friend was damn hard. "Sorry,
man. I'm not trying to offend you," Imamu said. "I—I
—well, I know a thing or two about life, myself, you
know?"

"I'm sure you do. And I didn't mean to offend you,
Imamu. . . ." They were like two little boys making up
after a fight. It made Imamu wonder why he had been so
upset. His mother was sick—almost dead from drink
when he had called the ambulance. That's why she was
still in the hospital. Still, to compare her illness to Iggy's
. . . "I—I'm gonna get a job when I finish the painting,"
he said. "That'll make things a li'l better, too. . . ."

"What kind of work do you want?" Olivette asked.

"Work work, man. Shoveling shit, if that's possible."

"Don't you have to belong to the union for that?"
Olivette asked. Their laughter washed away the tension.

"Of course, illness of that sort can be cured," Olivette said with a disarming assurance, to wipe out any traces that might be left of Imamu's anger. "But you can't take her out of the hospital and bring her back to this. . . ." His eyes swept the block. Imamu looked at Butler and Babs, half-asleep in the entrance of the cave, while their little boy played with some older kids. And it seemed to Imamu that this man-child, who saw everything, judged nothing, and was so full of himself, had to have more answers than he gave out.

"How?" he asked.

"She must believe in perfection," Olivette said with his saintly smile, the darkening of his golden eyes. "She must get to know about this vast area within herself. She must be helped to work with it, pull it out of herself."

"Perfection!" Imamu's hopes died. At the top of the stoop he turned to look at Olivette's face below him.

"Perfection," Olivette repeated. "Inspire her. Force her to believe. . . . Make belief in herself consume her. . . ." The penetrating eyes made Imamu feel uneasy.

"Man, is that what you think you doing with Iggy?"

"Isn't it worth a try?"

For a moment Imamu's mind fumbled. Then he thought about Pierre, his own uneasiness with the boy. But not wanting to seem to be testing Olivette, he answered, "I suppose your old lady is into all this perfection stuff?"

"Mother? Heavens no. Mother's too busy seeking."

"Seeking what?"

"Happiness," Olivette said with a laugh that exposed all his perfect white teeth.

"What's wrong with that?"

"Everything." Olivette seemed delighted to get the

chance to say, "Except that to her happiness depends on someone else. And of course that kind of thinking prevents self-searching."

"You're a hard man, Olivette," Imamu said.

"Not at all. There was this friend of Mother's who always said—"

But Olivette never finished, because someone had come out of the door behind him. Imamu turned and found himself looking into a familiar face.

"Well, well, if it ain't my old buddy John Jones. I knew I hadn't seen the last of you. . . ."

Detective Otis Brown—formerly of Brooklyn. A man Imamu had hoped he would never see again in life. "I hear you're taking up sprinting as your new career. I just hope you got enough wind left to come to headquarters and tell us what you did with that bag my men saw you holding."

8

Anything they wanted to know about his movements, he was willing to tell. The trouble was, he didn't know. "Man, it dropped somewhere. If it was still out there now, wouldn't I have found it?" Imamu kept explaining —had been explaining for hours. But Otis Brown's full, round, brown face, with its heavy moustache, remained impassive. Folding over the collar of his yellow starched shirt, a roll of fat—an addition since he had last seen the detective—made him look like a bulldog on the scent. His hard eyes glanced from Olivette to Imamu and back, as though he were set to jump at any signal.

Brown's white partner, Detective McCaully, had his six-foot frame slouched down in a chair, his feet on the desk, pretending to be asleep. But Imamu knew that beneath the cover of his lowered lids, he was studying them.

"Paint. . . ." Brown scoffed. "What you doing with a bag of paint, Jones?"

"Man—all you got to do is go up to the apartment. If you was there like you say, you got to have smelt— something."

"We've had our eyes on you for days, Jones."

"Not me, uh-uh, not me." Imamu shook his head,

holding tight to his anger. "I ain't been nowhere where you can see me—'less you got X-ray eyes. . . . And why me? Why it got to be me? Whatever you hauled me in for got to be heavy—and you got to know I ain't into nothing that got weight."

"We don't know that. We been hearing things."

They hadn't mentioned what they had heard, or why they had pulled in Imamu and Olivette. Imamu knew it had to do with the phantom burglaries that Al Stacy stayed so burned up about. But if he hinted that he knew this, big Brown would be on him. So they sparred, hitting here, hitting there, with Imamu hoping that Brown might leak a soft spot of knowledge.

"Where'd you say you was coming from?" Otis Brown asked again.

"Just go on and call the hospital, man. . . . I ain't saying no more."

Imamu wished he could let out a string of curses at the detective. But Olivette was sitting there listening. And too, they were in the precinct at the mercy of two six-footers. The one bit of comfort—they hadn't separated him from Olivette—pointed to the fact that they were merely fishing. And they hadn't taken them downtown to police headquarters.

"So—you split when you saw my men coming to question you—all because you had some paint you wanted to hide."

"Man. . . ." Imamu fought to keep his lip from turning into a sneer. "All over this city cats are out jogging, but when a dude jogs in Harlem, it's shooting time."

"Hold, hold it, Jones. Nobody touched you two."

Up to that moment Olivette had been sitting, looking,

and listening politely. Now he stood. "Are you two gen-
tlemen charging us with a crime?"

On hearing Olivette's voice, its well-modulated tone,
the attitude of the two men changed. Brown's eyes went
cautious. McCaully's feet slid from the desk. They
looked at Olivette with something like respect, even as
they looked down at his sneakers, the blue jeans, the
white turtleneck shirt, the watch on his wrist. He and
Imamu were dressed almost alike but the difference in
their speech marked them as being worlds apart.

"Well now." Brown spoke carefully. "I hear you're
new around the block."

"Yes, I am," Olivette said, looking directly at Brown.
Brown's shoulders moved uncomfortably. "We—my
family recently arrived from East Saint Louis. The name
is Larouche—Olivette."

"Why did you all decide to move to a place like
Harlem?" Brown asked. Olivette's head snapped up, his
eyebrows raised, his eyes flashed.

"Charge us or let us go," he said. Brown and Mc-
Caully exchanged glances. McCaully leaned over his
desk.

"You're pretty light on your feet yourself," he said.

"Are you talking about my running today—or rather,
yesterday afternoon?" Olivette pointedly looked at his
watch. It was after one A.M. "I usually am much better,
but for some reason, yesterday I found it difficult to keep
up with Imamu."

McCaully sat back. "One of the smart guys. Why did
you run when you saw the police coming?"

"Police? Oh—I didn't see them. Imamu decided he
wanted to run, so I ran along. Is that the charge?"

"Hey look." Brown got up, belligerent. The telephone rang.

McCaully answered. He grunted into the phone, then handed it to Brown. Brown talked into the receiver, his eyes moving from Olivette to Imamu, then back to Olivette, his manner changing. When he put the phone down, he looked less a bull and more a terrier. "We're letting you go this time," he said. "But don't think you're getting away with anything."

"Was that Mother?" Olivette asked. "Or her lawyer?"

"The smarties," McCaully snorted. Imamu and Olivette walked out.

Imamu stood on his corner, watching Olivette disappear in the dark going toward his block. Suddenly the one place he didn't want to go was home, to the heavy smell of paint. He saw a picture of himself as he must look painting the apartment. He hated the sight. How stupid, how stupid. He went instead to the park.

"Smoke, smoke. . . ." A figure emerged from the darkness as he entered.

"On credit?" he asked.

"I ain't said a drag, man. I said a smoke. . . ."

"If I can owe. . . ."

"You got to be sick. . . ."

The park, so empty by day, so alive at night, with the zombies coming out, stretching into wakefulness that would keep on until the rising of the sun.

Walking through the breathing darkness spotted by the glow of cigarettes and pot, Imamu retraced his steps to the boulder where he had been with Olivette earlier. He stretched out, looking up at the moon, the clear sky.

Lonely. He had thought of Gail while at the precinct,

of the Aimsleys. But he hadn't wanted to call the
Aimsleys. He hadn't wanted to shout help, help, help like
a broken record. He knew Mrs. Aimsley wanted to help
him. But why couldn't he be just an ordinary cat, taking
care of his mother, instead of being a nonperson taking
care of another nonperson? Why did he always need the
help of an outsider? Tears came to his throat—stuck
there. . . .

This was the first time he had seen or heard of Detective Brown since Perk Aimsley's disappearance. Brown
had pulled him in that time. He and his partner had
turned Imamu every way but loose. They had beaten him
with a rubber hose; then they had taken an ax and had
hit him on his neck as though trying to behead him.
Blood had spurted. Only as it turned out, the ax had
been rubber, the blood, tomato catsup. Imamu had been
scared almost witless. Now there was Brown again, turning every plan Imamu had made into the plan of a clown.
Doing tricks to call himself human.

Imamu knew the only reason he had been turned
loose, this time, was because of Mrs. Larouche's telephone call. It was certain that Pierre had heard what had
happened and had gone to her. Did that mean Brown
was through with him? No, it only meant that Brown
had it in for him. First, because Imamu had shown him
up by solving Perk's disappearance, and now, because he
and Olivette had exposed him as a fraud for pulling them
in. The stud was a sadist.

Sunlight woke him up. Bright nine-in-the-morning sunlight. Imamu stretched, looking around the empty park.
What in the devil was he doing out there? The park in
the mornings belonged only to the winos, out on the

benches, and the joggers, stretching their limbs on the sidewalks around the park.

Looking out toward the avenue, he saw that Al Stacy's players were already bunching up waiting for him. He walked down the hill and made it home.

In the apartment he brushed his teeth, washed his face, then went right out. Going into the shell of the building beside his, Imamu walked through, kicking rubble and empty bottles from his feet, searching through the sleeping junkies for Butler. He found him, still sleeping, his little boy curled up between him and Babs.

"Hey, man," Imamu called, shaking Butler. "Got some talk for you. . . ."

Butler lay still, so still Imamu thought he was dead. And Babs and the baby, too. Imamu knelt beside them, feeling for Bab's heartbeat, then felt for the baby's. But as he reached for Butler, the man threw a protective arm around his family. Imamu breathed in relief. He really didn't know how to feel for beats. But even not knowing, he knew that theirs ought to be beating heavier.

"Hey, man," he called, shaking Butler. "Get up. Got some talk. . . ."

Butler didn't move. Neither did Babs, neither did the baby. He shook Butler again. If anything was wrong with his family, he was the one who ought to check it. "Butler, Butler. . . . What's wrong with Babs?"

Butler snapped awake, looking at his wife, his son, out of reddened eyes. Then he looked at Imamu. "Whatcha talkin'—man. . . ." Then turned over and went back to sleep. Imamu yanked him up, tapping him on his cheeks. Finally Butler opened his eyes. "Man—you crazy or something? What you want. . . ?"

"Seen Omar?" Imamu asked.

"What I be doing seeing Omar?"

"I mean, he been into any loot lately . . . ?" Imamu felt a loosening of his tension, as their talking disturbed Babs. She roused herself enough to pull the kid close.

"Loot?" Butler said. "Only thing Omar is into is religion. Man, you waking me up at this time of the morning to ask them simple-assed questions?" Then suddenly Butler sprang to life. "What? Omar got loot?"

"I don't know. That's what I'm here asking."

Omar and Butler were the two guys capable of the phantom jobs—or they were at one time, before Butler got on drugs. But Omar might be using his religion as a cover. Butler would know. Junkies had a keen sense for folks with an extra dollar. Imamu looked down. He had to take it easy. If Omar wasn't the one, he didn't want Butler to be hitting him—or telling him that Imamu was asking. "Look, man," he said. "Talk to you later—when you about."

Then going out, he joined Al Stacy's customers, waiting for the gambler to show. Al Stacy came, parked his car. But Imamu waited for him to get done with business before going to him. "Seen you standing back there, Youngblood, what can I do you for? Need more loot?"

"No, man—need some talk," Imamu answered.

"Yeah—hear you and your boy got snatched yesterday. Them studs got to be kidding."

"They didn't act like it. What's really happening, Al Stacy? Why those turkeys really think studs from around here's to blame?"

"Whomsoever it be been leaving a wide open trail to Harlem. In Harlem pawn shops, with big-time Harlem hustlers.

"Pulled in everybody who's been in the can, who they

got a file on, who they think they should have a file
on—the list, man. . . . Tell you, those turkeys don't take
it light when black studs hits ofeys."

"And you don't—"

"Know—no. And if they hurt my business, if they
pulls me in . . . like I say, when I hurts I hollers—so I
ain't asking to know."

"Who do you think?" Imamu asked stubbornly. "It
just might be an ofey, trying to put black folks in the
wrong. . . ."

"I don't think about these things, Youngblood. I either
know something, or I don't. And in this case if I knew
I'd holler."

"What about Butler? He used to be the greatest."

"Hell, it ain't no junkie," Al Stacy said. "They'd have
long caught up with a junkie."

"Why not a junkie? Those dudes get slicker and slip-
perier as their need gets bigger."

"Yeah, they can climb up some slick walls—stuff like
that. But they gets anxious. Leaves clues. Whomsoever it
is, is a cool turkey. He's leaving the man sorely ignorant.
They don't know when or how or in what direction this
stud's working. That's why they pulling everybody and
their pappies in." Al Stacy walked in little circles, sock-
ing his hand with his fist. "And that's why they gonna
eventually—now I said eventually—pull me in. See,
Youngblood, the way they figgers, if it was whites, they
wouldn't have found nothing on account of whites who
go into places like those—got some good fences, see.
This dude, whomsoever he is, must still have most of the
loot he took. But he lets a li'l go here, a li'l go there—to
keep hisself going—until he finds a fence—or maybe just
to keep the law guessing."

"What about Omar?"

"Omar! Cra—p. . . ."

Al Stacy knew most of the guys around. Even without knowing them he knew them. Habits, styles. Somehow they gave themselves away—if they were pulled in, or out on the loose, they formed some kind of pattern that Al Stacy knew about.

"Al Stacy, where do I find out about the places this dude's been hitting. . . ."

"In the newspapers," Al Stacy answered. "In all the newspapers."

"Got any around?"

"Newspapers? What I be doing saving them things?" Al Stacy asked. "Want to find out, go to the library— that's what they got libraries for. Got one downtown— Forty-second Street. . . . Got everything you can ever want to know."

Imamu walked away wishing he could see Olivette before he went downtown. But he had never been invited to his friend's house. Ten o'clock. Maybe he could make it down and back before . . . ?

Imamu found himself walking toward the subway. The library had to be as good a place to pass the time as any.

9

It was almost three o'clock when Imamu came back up-town. He went directly to Olivette's and rang the bell. He rang again, before the woman on the street floor looked out. "Who do you want?" she called. Imamu looked down at the woman, standing on the side of the stone steps looking up at him.

"Larouche," he said. "Olivette—tall, good-looking."

"Two long and two short," the woman said and disap-peared into her apartment. Imamu stood looking stupid for a few seconds before he realized she had been talking about the bell. He rang—two long and two short—then waited. He was about to ring again when Olivette opened the door.

"Imamu. Where have you been?"

"To the library—Forty-second Street," Imamu said, excited.

"Oh. Have you seen Pierre—and Iggy?"

"No, man. I told you I've been downtown."

He had expected Olivette to invite him in. Instead Olivette came out, closed the door, and led him down-stairs. "I expected Pierre to wait for me," he said. "I had to go out."

They walked up toward the avenue, and Imamu, noticing Olivette's preoccupied expression, said, "I been looking into these cases—you know, the one they call the Phantom Burglar . . . ?"

"Yes?" Olivette said, absently.

"Yeah. Trying to find a pattern, man—one what's got these cops' mind blown."

"And what do you do when you find it?"

"Walk the streets—like a citizen." Imamu smirked. Olivette looked at him blankly.

"Don't tell me that you actually are thinking of trying to solve those cases?"

"I bet that I—that we can do as good as the lawmen, Olivette. Hell, when they go pulling us in—they just way off base. I can do better." Imamu didn't know why he hesitated telling Olivette he had solved a case Brown hadn't been able to. Maybe because he wanted to leave the title of perfectionist to Olivette.

"Really—now that might be interesting," Olivette said, showing a trace of excitement. "How do we start?"

"Well, I read all the newspaper stories—see? I got the places all written down here. . . ." He took a note paper from his pocket to show the addresses he had copied. "The dude's been working the scene—starting at those doormen apartments, near Fifth Avenue, in Harlem, then down to the Columbia University area. And now he's moved down to them swank neighborhoods—along Fifth Avenue by Central Park. I got to hand it to him," Imamu said in admiration. "He ain't no small-time—if he's really a brother, man."

"Are you really more interested in this Phantom, who's ripping off wealthy people, who probably are— excuse me—well protected by insurance, as well as the

law, than in this?" They were on the avenue and he
pointed to Stuff Smith, and his suntanned boss, driving
by in their white custom-made limousine, with its Lincoln Continental back and Rolls-Royce front, to where
their jostling junkie crowd waited for them.

"I don't take it lying down when I get pulled in for
something this joker's doing," Imamu said.

"And you feel it your lawful duty to do something
about it?"

"Man, these cops don't know from nothing, Olivette. I
could show them a thing or two—or three."

"I had been hoping we could finish up the apartment,"
Olivette said. "But if this is what you want—I had never
thought of detective work. It might be interesting."

"Maybe I'll have a great influence on you."

"You are a lovely person," Olivette said, smiling.
"And I might be quite good at it, you know."

"When do you think we can start?" Imamu asked. But
Olivette's interest had shifted. Looking up the block,
Imamu saw Iggy and Pierre coming toward them. They
were walking fast, talking to each other with excitement.
Imamu could feel the quiet spreading within Olivette as
he stood waiting for them to walk up—waiting for them
to see him.

They were almost upon them when Pierre saw Olivette. He turned as though to run back, stopped, then
came toward them more slowly, his hands twisting each
other. How strange that Pierre was so terrorized by his
brother. Iggy, too. His face twisted into a mixture of
arrogance and belligerence when he saw them. His eyes
darted around, searching for escape. But he too walked
up to them.

"Where have you been?" Olivette asked. Pierre, his

eyes growing big, stood silently. "Did you hear me,
Pierre?" Imamu realized that however confident Olivette
seemed, he did have fears of Pierre going places with
Iggy.

"We been—around," Iggy said, a sneer on his face.
"We been doing what we damn well please. Now what's
wrong with that?"

But Olivette's eyes were concentrated on Pierre, holding him where he stood, wiggling. And Iggy, seeing that
he wasn't the victim of Olivette's attention, twisted his
cap on his head, hunched his shoulders, and crossing the
street, called back to them, "I go where I please, get it?
And I do what the hell I wants. . . ."

"Mother didn't know where you had gone," Olivette
said to Pierre. "Go home and let her know that you're all
right."

Pierre nodded. He sprinted away, putting the crowd
between him and his brother.

Imamu swallowed his I-told-you-so that surely would
bring a denial by Olivette of the reason he was disturbed.
He wanted to tell Olivette, that whatever he thought, he
had lost control of Iggy. Imamu was sure of it. But would
Olivette admit it? He had better before they did something really wrong. Then recalling the fear on Pierre's
face, the twisting hands, Imamu prayed that something
hadn't already gone wrong. . . .

"Where were we?" Olivette asked, his eyes still following Pierre. "Oh—Imamu, can we talk about this tomorrow? I think I ought to go home to look after Pierre."

Imamu opened his eyes to the sunlight of his mother's
curtainless room. Turning on the radio at the side of
the bed, he let the music push him away. He lay, looking

up at the unfamiliar cleanliness of the ceiling. His time in
the precinct, his sleep in the park, had wrung him out.
The day before he had awakened early, but had lain in
bed waiting for Olivette's ring. When he hadn't come,
Imamu had simply slept through the day.

Now, looking around the room, Imamu doubted he
would finish the apartment. His mother? He imagined for
the hundredth time, taking her from the hospital, then on
the subway, bringing her into the apartment—a half-
painted apartment. Depression smothered him. Actually,
only the hallway and kitchen remained to be finished.
But it might as well have been the entire place, for the
effort it took him.

The music on the radio stopped. The news announce-
ment claimed Imamu's attention: ". . . the latest in the
long series of burglaries perpetrated by the elusive Phantom Burglar has finally resulted in violence. . . . The
victim, Mr. A. E. Auerbach, was found late yesterday
afternoon in his Fifth Avenue apartment by his secre-
tary, who had become alarmed when Mr. Auerbach did
not arrive for an appointment. . . . Arriving at his em-
ployer's apartment, he found Mr. Auerbach, his head
severely beaten, in a state of unconsciousness. Mr. Auerbach was rushed to . . ."

Imamu switched off the radio. The picture of Pierre
and Iggy, the last time he had seen them, flashed before
his eyes. He shook his head to brush it away. Iggy, the
Phantom? Violent, yes. But Phantom? Pierre . . . ?
Imamu thought of his lean, slinking body, the long slender hands. . . . He shook his head again. The police
pressure on him, his decision to investigate the crime,
were playing with his mind. Never. They couldn't
have. . . .

And a rich Fifth Avenue type! It was sure the heat would be on—if the police were still thinking the Phantom was from Harlem. Nine o'clock! Imamu jumped out of bed and made for the shower. He pushed aside his hope of Olivette's working with him. Olivette got started too late in the mornings to suit him.

But as he rushed downstairs, he met Olivette on his way up. "What you doing about this early, man?" Imamu asked.

"I could ask the same question," Olivette replied. "Where are you off to?"

"I'm getting on with the—with our investigation."

"Are you serious?"

"Never more in my life, Olivette. You hear what happened? A cat on Fifth Avenue got hurt. What if he dies?"

"How do you know it's the same?"

"The Phantom Burglar—the radio said," Imamu insisted.

"What can you—we do about it?"

"Find out who, that's what. I know these guys—how they operate. The minute I fall onto a pattern. . . . I ain't the dumbest guy around, you know."

"I know," Olivette agreed, smiling, and putting an arm on his shoulder, they went down the stairs. "And when we find out—what do we do? Turn the culprit over to the police?"

Imamu hadn't thought that one out. His feeling for Brown—which extended to his partner, McCaully—didn't jibe with turning in a human being to be messed over. "Look," he said. "I know one thing. I don't intend to be arrested for killing a sucker I haven't even seen."

"How can that happen?" Olivette said with a laugh. "You've been reading too many comic books."

"You seem to forget that all I did was go to the hospital to see my old lady and got hauled in for carrying a bag of paint. The law is just like addicts, man. They go crazy when they gets desperate."

"What about the apartment, Imamu? When do we get finished?"

"Later, man. Right now I can't do one other thing— not while these suckers are on my back."

And the police were thick on the streets, cruising, standing on the corners. Imamu knew that all over Harlem it was the same.

"Where do we start?" Olivette asked. Imamu pulled out the paper on which he had written the addresses of the burglaries. "The dude started here." He circled the address of a Harlem apartment. "And ended here." He wrote down the name of the morning's victim and "Fifth Avenue."

"Now, every day or so the cat hits a place not more than seven or eight blocks apart—working his way down. Why? I'd say that he cases his next job after he finishes with one. That's why they're so close. See the pattern developing?"

"Couldn't it be before?" Olivette asked.

"Not likely," Imamu said, satisfied that for the first time he sounded more knowledgeable than Olivette.

"And then . . . ?"

"I don't know," Imamu answered, irritated. "One step at a time. Let's get Auerbach's address from the phone book and go downtown. We can work our way back up."

The large white thirty-story structure on Fifth Avenue facing Central Park was awesome with its concrete-contained flowers at its sides, doorman in front hailing taxis for residents. So Imamu walked boldly through the door. Olivette followed. But as they stepped into the coolness of the carpeted lobby with its marbled walls, another doorman stepped out of a cubicle to confront them.

"Is there something I can do for you?" he asked.

"Well . . ." Imamu wondered why he hadn't put on shoes, instead of sneakers, to do his investigation. He reached for a toothpick then thought better of it. And deciding honesty had to serve him, he said, "Yes—we—we want to have a look at the Auerbach apartment—the one in which the crime was perpetrated?"

The doorman blinked, his eyebrows went up, and an astonished smile spread slowly across his face. "Do you have an interest in the case?"

And why hadn't he thought of a tie? Did he have one? He looked at the red and black uniform before him. He hoped the man hadn't read about criminals returning to the scenes of their crimes. Having decided on the truth, he answered, "Yes, a great interest. I—I'm helping out on the case."

"Oh?" The smile broadened. "I'm sorry, sir. I can't let you up," the doorman said, politely—so politely and so simply that they were out of the building and walking up the block before Imamu realized that they had really been kicked out.

"Do you really think that's the way to go about it?" Olivette asked. "It does seem a way to draw unnecessary attention to us—don't you think?"

"Maybe we don't look the part—exactly," Imamu agreed. And when they came to the next Fifth Avenue building on the list, instead of marching in, they stood outside looking it over. "Do you think we should go in . . . ?" Olivette asked.

"Maybe we should try tomorrow. . . ." Imamu said. "Maybe we should dress different." They walked on and Imamu said, "Whoever the cat is, he sure got a hell of a technique."

"How is that?" Olivette asked.

"Know that, and we got him," Imamu answered. But doubt had begun to build as he looked around the unlittered streets, almost empty except for the doormen. Elegant. No one he knew, or could think of, belonged in the league that would hit one of these buildings. They were too swank, too well guarded. From what he had read, all the burglaries had been on the upper floors. And no two buildings adjoined at the roof. Imamu gave up. He decided to go back home and see to his apartment. Nevertheless, he said:

"Way I see it, the dude's got to be something between a cat and a spiderman. He works his way down from the roof."

"On those high buildings? Wouldn't that be an unnecessary chance to take simply to impress the police?"

"Impress the police?" Imamu said. "Man, that dude's getting rich! He's into heaps of money! The way I see it—"

And then they were surrounded. Squads of unmarked police cars came at them from all directions. Big, muscled plainclothesmen, hippy squads—all running toward them. Imamu felt himself grabbed and pushed against a car, his hands forced to the top as other hands patted him down. And all the while, he kept hearing a shrill voice shouting, "That's them. They're the ones. I saw them. I'd know them anywhere."

Imamu twisted his head around, and before it was shoved down again, he glimpsed a tall, thin blonde, in a long dressing gown pointing. "Yes, yes—I saw them with my own eyes."

"What's she talking about?" Imamu shouted. "What's she—"

"Shut up and get in the car," someone said. "You'll get your time to talk—all the time you need. . . ."

10

He had been looking around the courtroom at the blonde who had pointed them out—sleek now in a tan summer suit. He kept looking around for the doorman of the Fifth Avenue building. And when he didn't see him, he looked back at the woman, feeling the hatred burning out of her face and eyes. And realizing that she was responsible for the net closing in around him, he looked at Brown until a movement in the back of the courtroom made Brown turn. Brown's eyes popped open wide. He sat up, tall, adjusting his tie, a simple look making his heavy face look comical. Imamu looked, too.

And there she came flaming down the aisle, her red hair blazing, her green eyes flashing. "How dare you? How dare you try to make a criminal out of my son? He's a saint. A future priest, and you're trying to make him into a convict. . . ."

"Your mother?" Imamu whispered to Olivette, sitting at his side in the dock.

"Yes—Mother."

"Wow. . . ."

"Lovely—isn't she?" Olivette said. The judge pounded with the gavel.

"Madam, I assure you I'm not the one who will make a criminal of your son. But I fear, if you don't sit down and be quiet, I'll settle for making one out of you."

"I know my rights," Mrs. Larouche shouted.

"I'm sure you will let us know all about them at your contempt-of-court hearing, madam," the judge said. Whereupon Brown left his seat and went to Mrs. Larouche to whisper in her ear. She turned on him, angry. Then her eyes went over him, measuring him. She wilted and like a child leaned against his broad chest, helpless. He led her to a seat.

The calendar was full that morning, with the arraignments of dozens of youths—mostly black and Puerto Rican, charged with everything from prostitution and loitering to stabbings. The two court-appointed lawyers had been busy giving them one minute per person before the court had opened. Imamu kept trying to look at them as they bounced up with renewed energy as each new case was called—asking for acquittals, or postponements, and dealing with the prosecuting attorney and judge for reduced sentences. But mostly Imamu kept looking at Brown and Mrs. Larouche—at his big head with its mixed gray hair, almost touching the red head. When lunchtime came, and the prisoners were being led from the dock back to the pen, Imamu looked back to see if they were leaving together. They were.

In the afternoon their case was called. Side by side, Imamu and Olivette stood before the judge, the lawyers hovering. Then as Mrs. Larouche came to stand beside Olivette, Imamu felt a sudden space behind him, as though a door had suddenly opened, into a pit which he might be drawn into.

"Are these the two suspects that you saw running

from your building on the day of the robbery?" the prosecuting attorney asked the blond woman, after she had taken her oath.

"They are."

"The charge, Your Honor, is suspected burglary and assault with a deadly weapon."

"You have heard the charges against your client, Olivette Larouche," the judge said. "How does your client plead?"

"Not guilty, Your Honor," Olivette's lawyer said.

"You have heard the charge against your client, John Jones. What does your client plead?"

"Not guilty, Your Honor," the lawyer repeated.

"What does the arresting officer have to say?"

One of the plainclothesmen who had twisted Imamu's arm came forward. "Your Honor, I was called by Mrs. Jan Austen, of the said address on Fifth Avenue, to the scene of the said burglary. There I apprehended two suspects, leaving the scene of the crime. We took them in for questioning, Your Honor, whereupon we understood that the two suspects had already been detained for questioning as suspects in the case of the Phantom Burglaries by Officer Otis Brown. . . ."

"Will Officer Brown please approach the bench," the judge said. Brown came up. After he took the oath, the judge asked, "Officer Brown, have you reasons to believe that these two young men have knowledge or are involved in the case of the Phantom Burglaries?"

Brown looked back at Flame Larouche, his shoulders moving uncomfortably. "I did detain the suspects, Your Honor, because we had reason to believe that they might have knowledge of the crimes committed by the Phantom Burglar," he said.

"And then the visit to the scene of the crime," the judge said. "What is your opinion, counselor?" he asked the district attorney.

"Your Honor, due to the seriousness of the crime— there is a man in the hospital—still unconscious, I recommend that the two suspects be remanded—"

"I object, Your Honor," the court lawyer said. "There has been no evidence linking my clients to this case, except the words of one hysterical woman."

"I am not hysterical," the blonde shouted, hysterically. "I know what I saw."

"Your Honor," the district attorney said. "To assure the prisoners' appearance in court, pending a hearing, I recommend that they be held in lieu of fifty thousand dollars bail."

"I object, Your Honor," their lawyer said. "Where are my clients to get that kind of money? The law has shown no evidence to prove a case against them. And as far as Olivette Larouche, who has no prior record, I consider that unjust and unusual punishment."

"Approach the bench," the judge said. And as the two lawyers approached the bench to have their whispered meeting, Imamu's knees buckled. Fifty thousand dollars! Were they mad! Had everybody in the world gone out of their minds!

"Very well," the judge said. "Bail to be set at twenty thousand dollars for each prisoner—or prisoners to be remanded in custody."

"I'll pay my son's bail," Flame Larouche said.

The judge looked up, surprised. And Imamu, seeing the reassuring look passing from Brown to Mrs. Larouche, looked vaguely around the hostile court as though expecting someone to shout out they had come

with his bail. And as the court remained amazingly silent, he realized that twenty thousand, as far as he was
concerned, was the same as fifty. A thrill of loneliness
curled his toes. Imamu looked away from the still-faced
onlookers as the guard touched his arm. But as he
started toward the dock, Olivette caught his hand,
squeezing his fingers. "Don't worry, Imamu, I'll have you
out. . . ."

Have him out? How did a nineteen-year-old, unem-
ployed, go about getting that kind of money? He looked
back at Brown and Mrs. Larouche, walking out with
Olivette, as though surrounding him with care. He shook
his head. Made no difference if he did have a gone-look-
ing old lady.

Then as the police van drove him to detention on
Rikers Island, Imamu wondered why he hadn't tele-
phoned the Aimsleys—or asked Olivette to call them.
But it seemed suddenly that he had been dodging being
hauled in for so long, he had come to believe that im-
prisonment was what he deserved—after the end of a
game.

Imamu was in the shower, the next morning, when he
heard his named called over the bubble: "Imamu Jones,
Imamu Jones. Come to Administration."

Who could that be? Had Ann Aimsley found out
about him and come? Had his name been in the newspapers, in connection with the Phantom Burglaries? On
the radio? Dressing quickly, Imamu went down to Administration. But only the small, pink, gray-eyed man sat
behind the desk. Imamu felt his pocket. No toothpicks.
He pushed out his mouth, moving his lips around, as
though one had already been placed between his lips.

"Jones, you've been bailed out," the man said. "Your lawyer will give you all the information on when you're to appear in court. . . ."

After leaving the main building, he got into the car that would take him over the bridge. His hopes rebounded and he tried to prepare just what to tell Ann Aimsley. How to convince her that, for real, he had nothing to do with Mr. Phantom, whoever he might be?

But when he got on the other side of the bridge, in Queens, Olivette stood there, grinning. And as Imamu walked toward him, he found himself grinning, too. Then they were running, grabbing each other, hugging—a moment of victory. Complete victory—victory for freedom, for love, for friendship. Imamu had to admit that although he had denied it, tried to push it out of his mind, he had expected this most perfect of friends to find the perfect answer.

Arms around each other, they walked toward a waiting car—a brown car—familiar. But before Imamu could figure out where he had seen it before, Otis Brown's broad face with its heavy moustache looked out at him.

"Brown!" Imamu's elation shrank.

"Yeah, man—it's me. . . ." Brown said.

Imamu slipped into the coolness of the air-conditioned car behind Olivette. He studied Brown's hair curling at the back of his hat, the thickness of his neck, folding over the starched yellow shirt collar. Whatever Brown's feeling for Mrs. Larouche, he still was the enemy. Imamu refused to be grateful to the enemy.

"You got a friend here, boy," Brown said, starting up the car. "Olivette sure went all the way in your corner.

So I expect you to keep your nose clean and your ass out of dirty water."

"Don't tell me you went my bail," Imamu said. A kind heart was one thing nobody could accuse Brown of having. Imamu thought again of the rubber ax, the catsup—his almost failed heart.

"Not exactly," Brown said. "What I did was get it reduced, and had you released on my recognizance."

Prickly sweat formed at the back of Imamu's neck. He didn't appreciate owing things to too many people—and Brown was the worst of them. "What do I owe you for that?"

"Now that ain't nice," Brown scolded. "I do you a good turn and—"

"I explained to Brown how we were working to solve the crime." Olivette laughed.

"Yeah," Brown grunted. "And I convinced them that you could be of help—more help outside—dig? Seeing it was you who helped solve that Brooklyn case, it figures that you think you're some kind of detective. But that was luck, Jones. Pure luck. Don't push it—you ain't."

Imamu pursed his lips around an imaginary toothpick. What damn luck? Insight—that's what he had that a thick head like Brown's couldn't come near to. The only thing that Brown could see about Perk's case was the quickest way to put Imamu under the jail.

"But as I told them," Brown said. "You got an inside track with the guys around the block—and I can use you. So—we work together, right?"

Imamu stared at Brown's thick neck. Was the guy for real? Did he expect him to act like a bird and sing? Forgetting that he had been investigating to do just that, Imamu answered Brown with a laugh.

"Anyway, you're out." Olivette turned and grinned. "Tomorrow we can get busy with the painting. But this evening Mother's invited you to dinner."

"Painting?" Brown said. "Don't be into painting so heavy you forget we got a deal, man. We got a date in court on the sixth of September. And what happens then depends on what you come up with."

The painting would all be finished by the sixth of September, whatever happened. But would he have to leave his mother alone? No. He had no intention of doing time—that was sure. But help Brown . . . ? Didn't he have to die and be born again?

That question kept bothering him. After he got home, he spent the rest of the day in bed, wanting to keep off the street. He was glad he hadn't had to call Ann Aimsley. Gail would never know that he had been in trouble again. But did that mean he had to help Brown?

The question was still disturbing him when he rang the bell to the Larouche house that evening. He rang twice before it opened—then there the lady stood, lovely. Lovelier close up than across a room. "Imamu," she said, greeting him with a red, wet-lip smile over white, white teeth. "I'm Flame Larouche. Olivette will be right back."

Imamu followed her upstairs, one flight, into the apartment, bursting with the smell of good food cooking. "Shrimp gumbo," she said, pointing to a pot steaming on a small burner on the table at the kitchenette end of the living room. She stretched out on the couch. Her green dressing gown made her eyes greener, her hair brighter. She wiggled her toes and Imamu had to admire the smallness of her feet, the obvious care. Her hands too were small, well-manicured; they appeared strangers to work.

But the place was clean. One room divided in two by the couch and drapes that were opened now. On the other side of the drapes was a queen-size bed. Bookshelves extended from wall to wall, into the living and dining room half, linking the two parts. On their side of the couch, a dinner table had been set, making of the entire room a lovely, comfortable apartment.

"Tell me about yourself, Imamu," she said, squeezing to the end of the couch, making space for him to sit. "Brown tells me you keep in trouble." She laughed, not believing.

It embarrassed him to sit by her, but it made him uncomfortable to refuse. He sat, hating to look at her, but unable to look away. Her thinness surprised him. Her soft look had given the impression of fleshiness. But it was only the way her breasts moved beneath her clothes.

"Pierre out, too?" he asked, to have something to say.

Her eyelashes fluttered. She threw him an apprehensive look. "Yes—boys, you know. . . . It's so hard to raise boys."

"Would you like to have a girl?"

She looked away, sighing. "Why talk about the impossible? I broke the mold."

So much seemed to lie behind that statement that Imamu waited for her to explain. Instead she let an uncomfortable silence develop. He stood up and went into the bedroom to study the books along the wall: *The World's Great Philosophers*; *The History of the World*; *Hellenic Civilization*; *Catholicism*; The Holy Bible.

"Wow." The soft shout came unbidden. "That Olivette is a heavy turkey."

"A genius," Flame Larouche said sarcastically, and at

Imamu's surprised look changed her tone. "He really ought to be in school—but—he's a genius." She smiled. "Do you have any influence on him, Imamu? He might listen to you. He does, you know—listen to people he likes."

"He'd make a great priest," Imamu said, thinking he was siding with her. She grimaced, her head bowed like that of a little girl. Then she looked at him and spat out, "Damn, hell, and all the dirty mother's-children." Then she sat back, pulling her face tight in mischievous satisfaction. "A priest? Oh, what a fantastic idea."

"But I th—" Imamu started when a movement at the door caught their attention. Olivette stood there, looking angrily at them. How long had he been there? Had he heard? And anyhow, what had they said?

But Olivette hadn't seen him until he moved. Then he said, "Imamu—I wondered if you'd remember. . . ." He came forward smiling. But his anger still hovered over them. Flame Larouche stood up then. She went to look at her gumbo, and for a moment Imamu thought of dodging Olivette's outstretched hands and following her to stand by her, to protect her. "Is everything all right?" Olivette asked. "Have you gotten over last night?"

"Last night?" Imamu said, forgetting.

"Yes—the night—or nights, in jail?"

"Oh—oh, yeah man. Took a little shut-eye. Bad trip. But from the smell of these grits . . ." he joked, breathing deeply, "it was worth it. Mrs. Larouche," he said, remembering, "you put up the money for my bail?"

"Sort of," she said.

"I want to thank you. . . ."

"Don't thank me," she said. "Olivette wouldn't have had it any other way."

The tone of her voice embarrassed Imamu. And as he tried to think of an answer, the bell rang. "Let me," he said, scooting in front of Olivette before he could get out the door. But he slowed his steps as he went down the stairs, taking his time to open the door, wanting them upstairs to lighten the air before he went back.

He opened the door for Otis Brown—looking newly cleaned in tan and brown, his face glowing, his shoes shining enough to blind—a bouquet in his hands but he outsmelled the flowers. "See you know about making time," Brown cracked. "Or didn't they feed you in the joint?"

Imamu had been thinking of Brown. Suddenly it came to him that cops were the ones with the inside track. What was wrong with being nice to Brown and finding out what he knew? So swallowing his wisecrack, and looking hard at the bouquet, he said, "Man, that lady rates diamonds."

"Oh—you noticed, too?" Brown said.

They walked slowly up the stairs, and when Brown stepped in, he filled the little apartment with his shoulders. He handed Flame the flowers, and looked around. Then he grinned at Imamu, and cocked his head at the book-lined wall. "You got a heavy friend here," he said, throwing wide his hands to include all the books, showing his pleasure at being allowed to be a part of a family that possessed that many books. "You got to be proud." He gazed at Olivette respectfully. Then taking off his hat, he laid it on the mantel of the never-to-be-used fireplace, and draped his jacket over a straight-backed chair. Rolling up his shirt sleeves, he nodded to Imamu. He was at home.

Olivette's eyes followed Brown's every move with such intensity that Imamu sensed that Olivette's earlier anger was because the man had overstepped invisible lines of conduct. And he grew sure when Olivette asserted his authority. "Are you comfortable, Brown?"

"Sure, sure."

"May I offer you something to drink?"

"I'll get it."

"No—let me. . . ."

"Okay, bourbon. . . ." Brown said. But it was obvious that he didn't get the message, because a second later he roared, "Where's the boy, Flame?"

"Please—not you, too," Mrs. Larouche gestured helplessly with a spoon. But Brown came back even louder:

"You listen to Olivette, Flame. The street's no place for a boy like Pierre."

"He can't be a prisoner in his house," Mrs. Larouche said.

"These streets are rough. You have—"

"But we live here, Brown."

"There are places to play—the park?"

"That's not dangerous?" Olivette looked at Brown, smiling.

"But even to go to—any park, he must go into the street," Mrs. Larouche said innocently.

"Well . . ." Brown wiggled uncomfortably. "Keep him nearer the house."

"This little house, Brownsie darling? It's so small. I do want to get the boys out of this little place—out of the slums. But—it's so hard. . . ." Her green eyes suggested held-back tears.

The lady wasn't playing for diamonds. She wanted to

settle in, and from the look of Brown, fumbling to make
an offer—any offer—she was ahead of the game—if they
could keep ahead of Olivette.

"Life is hard, Mother. And it becomes so much
harder when families don't cooperate—don't you agree,
Brown?" Olivette asked.

"Oh—sure—sure. . . ."

"But I always cooperate," Mrs. Larouche said angrily.
And seeing Imamu's surprise, she got back on track.
"You see, Brownsie—they're all I have—my boys. . . ."

And as though she had been listening, and hearing
where the rest of them hadn't, she said, "Ah, there's my
baby now. . . ." And Pierre opened the door. He came in
and stood with his back to the door, gazing at Olivette,
until Olivette turned his back on him, releasing him. Olivette walked to the bookcase at the foot of the bed,
pretending to be looking over his books. And Pierre
walked over to his mother and leaned against her. Mrs.
Larouche slipped a protective arm around him, but let
her arm drop when Olivette said, "Time for dinner,
Pierre. Go and wash up."

Pierre started out of the room but stopped when
Brown said, "Boy, where the hell you been? Now, I know
your brother tells you not to be hanging out in those
streets. . . ." Pierre stood looking from his mother to
Olivette, waiting.

"Wash your hands," Olivette said and Pierre faded out
of the door.

The gumbo was great. Imamu, whose diet consisted of
sandwiches, Kentucky fries, and Big Macs, had never
tasted anything like the gumbo, made up of okra, crabs,
shrimps, spinach, and tomatoes. He ate until his hand

collided with Brown's as he reached for his third helping. Then he stopped. The big man kept on eating. The top of his pants was unbuttoned to make room, and he kept wiping the sweat of pure pleasure from his face with an oversize handkerchief.

"Jones," he said, leaning back in the chair when he had finished. "Ain't this the life? Having a sweet mama to come home to—one who can cook this g-ood." Imamu kept his eyes averted at the obvious offer. He could understand Olivette's aversion to Brown. A big, good-looking man—one supposed brave—but so coarse —and a cop. A goddamn cop. . . .

They had been waiting for Brown to finish, but his words brought them all to their feet—Olivette to clear off and close the gate-legged table, pushing it to the wall, Pierre to wash the dishes, and Flame Larouche to relax on the couch.

"And you don't find it strange, Brown," Olivette said, "that simply being out on the streets exposes us to so much?" Imamu and Brown blinked at the revival of the long-dropped subject.

"That's where trouble happens, man," Brown said. "The streets. . . ."

"We know." Olivette used his polite smile. "We had the experience, didn't we, Imamu?"

"Well, you know—it was one of them things," Brown said. "We didn't really get a good look at *you*," he said to Olivette. But his eyes went instinctively to Imamu. Instead of hitting back, Imamu took a toothpick from the little glass on the coffee table.

"But trouble did happen," Olivette insisted. "And the last time it wasn't even on these streets."

"Son—you can't blame us," Brown said. "With the

kinds of things been happening. . . . Anyway, white folks can't tell the difference in colored folks."

"What kinds of things, Brown?" Imamu asked, ignoring the last remark. "We been picked up for something we don't know about. Least you can fill us in."

Flushed from his joy at good eating, relaxed, Brown even looked generous leaning back on his chair. "All I know is, it's likely a dude from Harlem's been doing the jobs. We don't know what he looks like, how he comes or goes, who he's likely to hit next. Our guess is that it's some ordinary joker from around—who did a long stretch and learned a new style and is trying to develop it."

"Why it got to be a black dude?" Imamu asked.

"He unloads stuff around Harlem. Not the real good stuff he makes off with. The so-so stuff. He must stash the rest, feeling his way to right channels. . . . We wants to nab him before he does."

"Anybody can unload stuff in Harlem," Imamu said. Just look at the junk being unloaded right out in the streets—in front of your precinct."

"That's another chapter, baby," Brown said. "We can't do nothing about that—know what I mean . . . ?"

Means you cops would have to do some real work instead of messing with guys like us, Imamu wanted to say. Instead, he said, "You got to have another reason to think he's from around here."

"The part we ain't let out," Brown said, "is that the dude—this Phantom Burglar—ain't that a number. . . . Hell, he started hitting the bigwigs, on the Terrace—on Lenox Avenue—right? It means that he's started where he had to have a place to just disappear. And he went in and out—and no one noticed him. . . . And he goes into places like pawn shops, and nobody seems to be able to point him out—now he can't be white—right?" Brown waited, and as no one said anything, went on. "And the cat's moving downtown—steady. Like he's trying to say to us, I'm doing this my way—all the way and what you gonna do? The way I figure, that Auerbach job was a slip-up. Auerbach wasn't supposed to be there. But Auerbach forgets something and doubles back. . . . Then he had to let him have it. No one else ever seen the stud—see. That turned out to be that sucker's big mistake. All hell's broke loose now—and if Auerbach dies . . . ? He-has-had-it. . . ."

"Probably a junkie?" Imamu asked.

"De-fin-ite-ly not. . . . Oh sure, a junkie can do most things. Climb up the side of icy Mount Everest if he needs a fix. But his desperation messes him up. Forces him to leave clues. This cat's cool. . . ."

"What about the woman who pointed us out?" Olivette asked. "She picked us—two of us—out. Yet you say it's the work of one person."

"A little messed up," Brown said. "You know with all the press. . . ."

"Hysterical, you mean," Olivette said. "Yet you arrested us?"

"Look, you all trying to make like detectives, ask this doorman some simple questions—naturally he calls us in. Then you go walking down the street like supermen—broad daylight. Well, the broad was looking out of her ground-floor window. And her house was the one hit the day before. Course she got hysterical—called the cops."

But Imamu refused to sit still for that one. "Man, we was two—two guys get thrown in jail. And I—I spent a couple of nights . . ."

"But you ain't in jail now, Jones," Brown said. "You ain't in jail."

"And we have you to thank for that, Brownsie baby," Flame Larouche said, stretching out, her voice sounding sleepy. "Children, aren't we just about the luckiest—to have a smart man like Detective Otis Brown around the house . . . ?"

11

The two-week heat wave had to break, Imamu thought as he walked home after dinner. A restlessness brought on by the heat had pulled women from the houses, had driven them to the sidewalks where they sat, dresses drawn up over knees, fanning themselves with folded newspapers. At the corner women and men stood in the strong blast of water pouring out of the fire hydrant, where screaming kids played. Plagued by a nagging feeling of something amiss, Imamu opened up the front of his shirt, hoping to catch a passing breeze.

Slipping in between the pages of his mind, a thought, an idea, refused to be pinned down. Or had it been something Brown had just said? He thought of going back, waiting for Olivette, to talk it out. But he really wanted to think it out alone. Because it did seem to him that he had to find the key to his own freedom.

He crossed the street, walked to his stoop and stood looking up to his floor, thinking of the empty apartment, waiting. It would be hot up there, hotter than the street because of the heat from the roof. He walked on by.

"Hey, Imamu. . . ." Butler shouted to him from the

corner. "Wait up." Jauntily, Butler walked up. Clean, free from the somnambulistic effects of a recent fix, or the agitation of his need for his next, he looked like his handsome, efficient self, better than Imamu had seen him for some time. Thin, too thin, and Imamu knew that beneath his rolled-down sleeves, Butler's arms looked pockmarked, as though from an ancient disease. And Imamu knew that whatever he said had to be a lie, a story put out for money to get his next fix.

"Hey, what's happening?" Imamu asked.

"Got a buy for you, man. What can you give me for this?" Butler pulled a ring from his pocket and showed it to Imamu. Imamu reached for it, to examine it, but Butler pulled it back. Imamu grew alert.

It had been a long time since Butler had handled anything of value—except perhaps gold chains he had snatched off unsuspecting chicks. But this ring was good —Imamu didn't have to look twice to see that. It was a gold ring with a diamond that was for real. "Man," Imamu said, cautiously. "You know I don't have no bread. . . . But if you want, I can get rid of it for you."

"No way—man, I got to hold on to this."

"You snatch it?"

"Found it." A lie. But Imamu cooled his interest.

"No jive? That's some find, man. Hell, you can get a mint for it. Go on and see Moe at the pawn?"

"Won't touch it. Says it's too hot."

Imamu let his mind run through places where Butler might have picked up the ring. He hadn't found it. He had taken it from someone. But from whom? Butler had run out of straight friends. No one could afford to trust him. Even his mother wouldn't let him near her house. A jewelry store with that kind of stuff would let him in only

under guard. Times get tougher and tougher for the
junkie.

On a chance, Imamu asked. "Hey, when you seen
Iggy? I'm looking for him."

"I seen him yesterday. Been by his house."

"Seen him today?"

"Naw. Ain't seen him." Then Butler's eyes got quick
with suspicion. "Why?"

"Iggy's my buddy. Ain't seen him in days. I been in
the lockup."

He walked on to the next corner, and turned it, heading to Iggy's. Walking mid-block, Imamu went into
what had once been a beautiful apartment house between
the park and Eighth Avenue. He ran up the flight of
stairs and knocked on Iggy's apartment door.

Then he waited, listening for sounds from inside. He
knocked again. Iggy had to be home. There were so
few places open to him. Imamu had just left Pierre at
home, and it was still too early for Iggy to have thought
up what else to do for the evening.

Iggy's mother worked, had always worked. And Iggy's
apartment—when he wasn't in jail—was his cage. Being
locked in when he was small had kept him in need of
being locked in. Imamu knocked, long and hard. Finally
he heard movement on the other side. "Iggy," he called.
"It's me, Imamu." The door cracked open; eyes stared
out over a chain. "What you want?" Iggy asked sullenly.

"I got some talk for you, man."

"What talk?"

"Since when you and me can't talk, Iggy? We been
buddies. What's with you?" Iggy kept looking at him
over the chain. Finally he removed the chain and opened
the door. Imamu pushed past him into the apartment.

"What the hell you want, Imamu?"

"I got some things I want to ask, man."

Imamu went down the hall into the living room—a
well-put-together living room with painted flowers covered with small rugs, starched curtains at the windows,
over the gates. Iggy's mother had always kept a neat
apartment, always with those gates, locking burglars out.
"Look, man," Imamu said to the suspicious boy standing, still at the door, looking at him through narrowed
sulky eyes. "You got to know I just come from jail—
bailed out."

"What's that got to do with me?" Iggy asked. Imamu
kept walking around the room; then he moved past Iggy,
going up the hallway to Iggy's bedroom. He stood looking around, sure that he was right, and Iggy's attitude
added to his certainty. Where would Iggy hide something
like jewelry? On the windowsill there were a few well-
read comic books. He looked at the dresser. But that's
the last place a cat like Iggy would think to hide something.

"You and Pierre been into lots of things of late," he
said.

"Things like what, man? Listen, Imamu, I don't 'pre-
ciate you just walking in my house taking over."

"Where'd you get that ring you give Butler yesterday?"
Imamu asked, guessing as much as anything.

The suddenness of his question caught Iggy off bal-
ance. His eyes rushed to his closet, then back at Imamu.
"What you talking about?" Imamu eased over to the
closet and with a sudden movement pulled the door
open. On the shelf he saw some clothes piled carelessly.
He started reaching for them, and suddenly Iggy stood in
front of him, his knife to his stomach.

"Hey, man." Imamu backed off. "This is me, Imamu. Your old-time friend."

"I ask what you want here, Imamu?"

"What you hiding up there, man? Or did Butler clean you out yesterday when he was here?"

Iggy moved his shoulders irritably, wanting to get to the closet. But he had already let too much out, so he kept his knife pointed at Imamu. "Get the hell out, Imamu. Go before I off you, man."

"Look, Iggy," Imamu said, talking fast. "I come to ask you a favor, man. My old lady's coming home soon, and here I get caught for some simple job, I swear."

"What's that got to do with me?" Iggy pushed his head out, reminding Imamu of his dream of rats pushing into rats.

"I don't know what it's got to do with you. But where were you and Pierre that day?"

"What day?"

"About three days ago—the day Pierre was supposed to be home and you all just went off."

"Don't know what day you talking about. I been home. Sick. Ask my mother. I been in this house sick."

"Hiding out?" Imamu asked. "What you done, man?"

"Who says I'm hiding out? I tell you I been sick. . . . What I got to hide out about . . . ?"

"That's what I'm asking you, man? I know you got loot from somewhere. But where?"

"If I do, it ain't none of your damn business."

"That's what I come to tell you, Iggy. You ain't got nothing. You been cleaned out."

Imamu kept studying the evil, closed face. Iggy's face had been evil since he was seven—but never had it been so completely closed. Not to him. Iggy had never been able to owe loyalty except to one person at a time. This sure wasn't his time.

Iggy kept looking at the closet, wanting to search it. And Imamu, wanting to know if he was right, even at the risk of a knife in his gut, said, "Go on, look. The stuff's gone, man. Gone."

Iggy reached up and snaked down the pile of goods, then moved his hand around the shelf. Wild-eyed, he began pulling everything down from the shelf. But he found nothing he was looking for. Then he looked at Imamu. "Get the hell outa here," he said.

"Ah come on, Iggy. We friends. All our lives we been friends. You owe me."

Eyes narrowed down to slits, Iggy stepped near to Imamu. "I don't owe you a damn thing, you hear me, Imamu? Not a damn thing. I don't owe you no more than I owed Muhammed." Imamu stepped back then, and knowing it would be his end if he showed fear said:

"Sure you do. We owe each other. You forget my old lady?" He hated using his mother to get himself off the hook. And having to use her made him angry with himself. It made him hate Iggy.

It worked. Iggy's eyes opened up a little—as though something had wormed its way through his twisted mind. He put the knife away. "I don't be owing you the rest of my life, Imamu Jones," he said. Shrugging, Imamu walked out of the room and out of the apartment, swaggering.

Outside in the hall, Imamu's knees buckled. Even though he knew Iggy was capable of anything, this was the first time he had actually been afraid of him. Knowing he had come as close to dying as he had ever been made him need to change the scene.

Leaving Iggy's building, Imamu kept right on walking to the subway. He caught a train to Forty-second Street, where he walked around the streets, then went to a movie which he sat through without seeing. Back uptown, on his way home, he still suffered from weakness in his knees. What if Iggy, in his twisted way of thinking, thought it was he, Imamu, who had ripped him off? Even Iggy had to know that the smooth, efficient way of smelling loot was part of a junkie's sickness.

Still, Imamu kept the lights out in the apartment when he went in. He didn't want Iggy to look up and see the light come up. In the dark of his mother's bedroom, Imamu looked through the window at the flow of restless bodies, walking around the half-lit streets, children running in and out of abandoned buildings, playing, screaming, happy. It might have been midday instead of way after midnight. He thought, suddenly, of Furgerson. How lucky to be out of it all, even if being out of it merely meant sneaking in and out on the way to and from work.

Leaving the window, Imamu threw himself across the bed. He lay staring through the darkness at the ceiling. Step by step he went over the events that had taken place since leaving Rikers Island that morning. So much, it had made the day the longest he had ever lived through.

If he had been right and the ring Butler had was one of those stolen by the Phantom, then a link had been established: Iggy. But if Iggy, Pierre too. Imamu thought of Iggy and Pierre when he and Olivette had seen them on the avenue. The guilt. Damn, he had warned Olivette about Iggy. Iggy wasn't a cat that stayed under anybody's control. Olivette was hard to reach when he had made up his mind.

Then, he might be wrong. After all, he had only

seen that one ring—in Butler's hand. How did Brown
know that the Phantom wasn't a junkie? Junkies did
some of the damnedest tricks—without training—when
they needed a fix. And Butler had been the slickest, best-
trained six-story man ever, before he had become an
addict. Iggy's acting up might not have anything to do
with the burglaries. After all—only the police thought
the Phantom was someone in the neighborhood.

Imamu felt tired. What had he set out to solve? Even
before he got started, he had landed in jail, and might be
messed up for life, judging from his buckling knees. With
the real test still to come.

He thought about Gail, stretched out on the hot beach
of a beautiful island. If he had a telephone, she would
have called him. But then, if he had a telephone, he
would have called Ann Aimsley. He regretted now not
having taken the train out to Brooklyn, to get to the
brownstone, to go up to his bedroom, to get into his bed
and let his foster mother come up to soothe what ailed
him. Even more than for Gail, he felt the need for her
mother.

He was about to get up, to go out and get on the train.
Then a grinding of brakes, the sound of steel hitting
steel, steel twisting into steel, the shattering of breaking
glass, the puncturing of tires, pulled Imamu up and back
to the window. Looking out into the street, made strange
by a sudden silence that had forced the restless bodies
below into stillness, Imamu saw the wreck of two cars on
the cross street of the avenue. Shocked, unable to think
of anything but a telephone, when he had no phone, he
stared out at the bodies hanging out of cars—bloody,
unconscious—at the bodies strewn around the street. He

tried to move, to run out to offer help, call an ambulance. But the horror of it held him.

Then a movement on the street below—slowly at first
as the figures moved out of their stillness. Slowly the
movement flowed toward the unconscious victims. Then
suddenly, like swarms of flies they were all over the
wreck, hovering over the cars, busy, intent. Imamu knew
what was happening and still could not move. Like giant
ants, pulling, tugging, at everything movable, they
worked. In the shortest space of time they were running,
running, leaving the figures, doll-like naked, askew on
the streets. And he stood there, stood there—then he
heard the sirens.

Needing the support of his mother's bed, Imamu
moved back. But his knees gave out. He slumped into a
heap on the floor beneath the window. Pulling himself
into himself, he shivered, kept shivering.

Hours later the doorbell rang. He looked up. Daylight.
He tried to get up. He had to get to the door. It might be
Olivette—someone. He needed someone to be with him
—to help him. The doorbell rang again. Imamu crept on
his knees, trying to rush himself, trying to get to the
door, before Olivette, before whoever it was, thought he
wasn't home.

Getting to the door, he managed a whisper. "Who—
who is it?"

"It's me, Mrs. Dawson, Imamu. Did you see Gladys?"

The sound of a familiar voice relieved him. Imamu
held on to the doorknob and pulled himself to his feet.
He opened the door. Mrs. Dawson, stood outside, bent,
gray, in a thin-strapped sun dress. "Where's Gladys?"
she asked him.

"Gladys? I ain't seen her."

"She's not home, Imamu. She ain't been home since the day before yesterday."

"Why me!" He heard himself shouting. "Why come to me? Go to the police . . . the hospital. Gladys must have been in that accident." But the bodies strewn over the street had all been white. Maybe the other car . . .

"Hospital? What accident? Oh my God . . ." Mrs. Dawson started screaming.

"I didn't say. I don't know. . . . I swear to God, I don't know." He fought against the sobs choking him. "All I know—she ain't here. . . ."

Maybe there had been no accident. Maybe he had been dreaming—having one of those stupid nightmares. . . .

"Help me. . . ." Mrs. Dawson's voice echoed the hysteria rising within Imamu. "Oh my God, help me, Imamu. Gladys is your friend. . . ."

"I got to think, Miss Dawson. Let me think. . . ." Imamu fought to keep his voice low, the tears from struggling into his eyes. "For God's sake, let me think. . . ." He closed her out. Then kneeling at the door, his forehead pressed against it, he opened his mouth to let the sobs tearing at his chest, his throat, rush out.

12

His tears drained and he still crouched shivering at the door, losing the pattern of his thoughts. He crouched, pulling himself into a near coma. He didn't know how long he'd lapsed when the jarring sound of the bell jerked him out of his numbness. He stared at the door, not knowing for a moment where he was.

Who was it? Why had they come? His mind turned slowly. He thought first of Iggy, Iggy's knife. The bell kept on ringing. "Imamu . . . Imamu. . . ."

Imamu blinked at the door, trying to match a face to the familiar voice. "Imamu . . ." The voice called loudly through the door. Imamu worked himself to his feet. He fumbled with the knob and lock, then opened the door a crack. Olivette pushed by him into the apartment.

"Where have you been, Imamu? I came by last night. I thought they might have pulled you in again. It's getting to be a habit," he joked, but his eyes, searching Imamu's face, showed concern.

"I—I . . ." Imamu's teeth chattered. His body still shook as though from a fever. He tried to steady himself, and leaned against the wall.

"You're not well," Olivette said, and helped Imamu to the front bedroom where he sat on the bed, nestled in its blue, false alcove.

"I—I—man, sure am glad to see you," Imamu said. "I—I needed you. I—I . . ."

"What's happened?" Olivette sat beside him. Unable to answer, Imamu hung his head between his legs. "Tell me," Olivette insisted. And when Imamu still didn't answer, he said, "Do you think that maybe—if we did some work—it would help you get yourself together?"

"Work . . . ?"

"If we finished . . . ?"

"Finish? Finish what?"

"Painting—we don't have that mu—"

"What the hell do I care about some damn paint?" Imamu burst out, letting his pain ease into anger. "I don't give a damn about one thing—least of all this damn apartment. . . ."

"Whatever is the matter?" Olivette moved to him, instead of away as Imamu had expected. "What happened, Imamu?" He put an arm around Imamu's shoulders and Imamu fought the desire to lay his head against the other's chest. Instead, he reached into his pocket for a toothpick, then threw it on the floor.

"Man . . . I seen something, last night—I never thought to see in my life. . . . An accident—right out there. . . ." He pointed to the window. "White folks. . . . At least in one of the cars. I didn't see those from the other so good. That one was so smashed up. . . . Olivette, nobody was around—police, I mean. . . . But then, there they all were—the cats out there, running over them, stripping them. . . ." Imamu's voice lost itself in the huskiness of emotion. He swallowed. "Olivette," he

cried, "they were like swarms of locusts—eating . . .
eating . . ." He shuddered. "Zombies out of a bad dream.
But I knew them all—once," Imamu cried. "They were
my boys. . . . Olivette, what's happening to us . . . ?"

Olivette sat quietly. Imamu cried. When Imamu had
stopped, he still sat, silently. When the agitation within
Imamu had subsided, Olivette said, "Okay, get washed
up. We're going out."

"Out? Where to?"

"Out in the streets—to take a walk. . . ."

"I can't, Olivette. I don't want to go out. I never
want to go out there again."

"Yes, you do. You will." Olivette put a distance between them, a father–child distance. He went into the
bathroom and turned on the faucet to fill the tub. "Go
on, get a bath and get dressed. We–are–going–out."

Imamu let himself be pushed. It was what he needed.
He wanted to listen to someone, to be told what to do, to
obey. He took his bath. When he came out, Olivette had
spread his clothes on the bed. "Just remember," Olivette
said. "Today is like all other days. What you saw last
night happens. Only you saw it."

When they stepped out on the stoop, clouds had appeared. A cool breeze was blowing. Descending the
stoop, Imamu kept his head high—to avoid contact, and
because Olivette had told him to. But Olivette kept looking into the bombed-out buildings, kept nodding to those
who nodded to them.

As they walked up the block, Imamu heard Butler's
voice: "Hey, my man. Let me hold a li'l something. . . ."

Imamu spun around, hostility staring out of his eyes.
A knowing look slid over Butler's—an answering hostility replaced his friendliness. What did he know? Butler's

eyes seemed to say. Who was he to condemn? Imamu's hostility changed to guilt. But he kept his voice harsh as he said, "That ring you ripped off Iggy got to have made you a fistful to hold on to."

Then he and Olivette walked to the corner, where they stood waiting for the flow of traffic to break. And traffic did flow from east to west, and when the light changed, from north to south. Normal. Everything like before! The sidewalks were filled with folks talking, walking! Had it all been a dream then? His imagination? Then he saw the chalk—bright yellow lines marking off the spots where bodies had lain.

"Crazy," he whispered, as though afraid to be heard by the police in the patrol car at the corner. "It's like nothing happened. But I saw it—I swear I saw it."

"Life flows on, Imamu," Olivette said. "That's why you had to come out and join it. If you had locked yourself in, you might never have been able to come out—to walk these streets again. After all, it wouldn't do for this detective team to break up because you were afraid."

The traffic flowing over the scene of the accident released Imamu from the worst of his terror so that he managed a little laugh. And as they walked by the crumbling buildings, with the haunting faces, shut into their own worlds of fantasies, Imamu reached for a toothpick. Finding he had none, they walked the few blocks to the corner stand, where he bought a box. Then they went to the park and made their way to what had become their spot. Lying beneath the big boulder—Olivette on his back, Imamu on his stomach—Imamu shook his head.

"So many victims," he said. "Victims, messed over, with only some yellow lines to mark where they passed."

"Which victims?" Olivette asked.

Surprised, Imamu looking into Olivette's face, saw only calmness. The dude hadn't been listening to him. Didn't he believe what he had said? "Man, I tell you I saw. Them suckers, man, stripped them bodies naked— left them out there . . ."

"But aren't they victims too, Imamu?"

"Who?"

"The addicts, Imamu. Don't you see them as victims?"

"You can't mean that, Olivette—not in the same way."

"But I do, Imamu."

"You didn't see this, man. I tell you they weren't like nothing human. . . ."

"They call it dehumanization," Olivette said. "But it's just a case of victims victimizing the victimizers, isn't it?"

"But those were innocent folks. . . ."

"Who is innocent, Imamu? Everybody is profiting from the swarm of locusts—as you call them. After all, money circulates. Houses are bought, landlords get rich, campaigns are paid for, presidents are elected—it all costs money. . . ."

"I don't dig you, man." Imamu shook his head. "You can't let them cats off the hook that easy."

"They're not off the hook, Imamu. You know that. They're out in the streets, hooked and bleeding to death. Most of them the waste of our inner cities. Nothing can save them. It's in the nature of things. Human waste affects us all. We are, after all, in the same world. Only there are those who don't seem to know it."

"Me neither," Imamu said. "All your talk about the sun being able to do most things sounds okay. But lots of folks out there—those others—believe in God. They don't know about what you talking about—and lots of them's been to college," Imamu said.

"And you're defending them?"

"Yeah. . . ."

"But they're not defending you," Olivette said. "They sit in their churches and pray for your death, along with the death of those locusts, swarming over filth. They've made us helpless to get out—and damned us to stay in."

"I can't believe that," Imamu insisted, wishing he had Gail there to help him handle Olivette and all that college talk.

"It's the contradiction of values, Imamu," Olivette said. "Contradiction of values left dangling like particles —can be confusing. . . ."

"Are you trying to defend those addicts, man?" Imamu asked.

"No—not really," Olivette said. "But I do know and understand that when men are hungry they must eat. Do you remember the book *The Survivors*? A plane wreck where survivors were forced to eat the dead?"

"That's not the same."

"Surely you've seen war pictures where soldiers raze villages, kill women and children to secure it—or get food," Olivette asked.

"You're talking about particular times of stress," Imamu said.

"But addicts are always under stress."

"No," Imamu said, shaking his head in despair. He thought about big Stuff in his flashy car, and the cool, gray-eyed white stud, and the addicts just waiting for

them to come. "Addicts have a choice, Olivette. They
can always walk, man. . . ."

"Not true, Imamu. Nobody can just walk away from
the life—or situation—they are condemned to. Everything is everything."

Imamu looked over the street, thinking about the nodding heads, Butler, the accident. What did it all mean?
Everything is everything? Would he ever understand Olivette fully?

"Have you always been this way, Olivette?" Imamu
asked.

"What way do you mean?"

"All this talking you do," Imamu said, sitting up and
pulling at a blade of grass to replace his toothpick. "Yet
I don't see you hanging with the cats."

"I happen to find more in you that I enjoy."

"But I belong down there. They used to be my boys,"
Imamu said.

"But you're not down there. You're up here with me
—scared, almost to death, by what you saw—and afraid
to get into trouble."

"I guess you're right."

"Under conditions like that, Imamu, isn't it hard to
think of perfection?"

"Oh, man, that's your thing," Imamu said, tossing
away the blade of grass. He pulled out another. "I ain't
into that."

"But what are you into? Trying to change that street?
If you do, you know you'll get wasted." He laughed at
his pun.

"You're the one sticking up for them."

"No, I'm not. I'm just pointing out—facts. If you

stand still, you will be consumed. You have to keep
fighting to stay ahead—so you might as well put up a
struggle for perfection."

An uneasiness touched Imamu. He and Olivette naturally looked at most things from different ends; still, Olivette sounded near the truth.

"Now your mother," Olivette said. "What will she do
when she comes home?"

"Look, I'd just take her as is, if she'd stay off the
booze."

"Then you must convince her that she can do something that no one else can do."

"How?"

"Do something—buy her seeds. Help her to plant,
flowers, fruits. Make her think that she's far superior to
those who drink and get drunk—make her believe in her
importance, until it's her habit to think she's important. . . ."

"What if the seeds don't grow?"

"They will—just tell her to use a little patience and
depend on the sun." Olivette laughed.

"You think that'll be easy?"

"No—but nothing is. I bet it wasn't even easy for you
to stay off drugs when your other friends went into it."

Imamu rested on his elbows and looked down into
Olivette's face. He held back the urge to touch its
smoothness. The cat was crazy—but so nice.

"No Imamu, I'm not crazy," Olivette said, reaching
up to touch Imamu's face, with a simple gesture that
took embarrassment out of the act. "For some fellows
on the block, it's too late. Too much has been done
against them. But you—for whatever reason—you're

saved. You should try to do more—perfectly. It's hard—but Imamu, most things are difficult."

"Has Pierre reached perfection?" Imamu said, suddenly, expecting Olivette's anger. Olivette sat up, his face closed.

"No—but he has come a long way. There are too many years between us. I managed to overlook him for a long time. Then there he was—breaking out like a wild, uncultivated seed. I had to look after him—bring him under control. No, Pierre hasn't reached perfection, yet —but he's come a long way. . . ."

Imamu let a silence hang between them, thinking of Pierre, his big, round eyes, the fear they showed when he looked at his brother, the way he sought his mother's protection. He let it hang, trying to force Olivette to admit, even to himself, that Pierre was not perfect, nor likely to become so.

"And your mother," Imamu said finally, "do you think she's reached the perfection you talk about?"

Olivette stood up, brushing dirt from his clothes. He stared down the hill, then at Imamu, and smiled. "Mother? You have to admit she makes perfect gumbo."

13

They walked quietly toward the avenue on their way home. Imamu kept thinking of Olivette, of his family, of Flame Larouche, her clear laugh, her childish cursing the evening of the dinner. Imamu liked her—more, he understood her. Having Olivette always around had to bring out feelings like that in people. It had nothing to do with liking or disliking the cat. It was the sacredness about him. The more respect you felt for the cat, the more you felt like hitting out. The trouble was, Olivette was a genius. And geniuses were just different people. . . .

"Wonder where Al Stacy is?" Imamu said, noticing that the usually busy corner was empty.

"Isn't that your friend across the street?" Olivette asked, nodding to Al Stacy, in his Cadillac about to drive off. Seeing Imamu, Al Stacy stopped the car, honked his horn, and called, "Come here, Youngblood." When Imamu had crossed the street, he asked, "Seen anything of Gladys?"

Only then did Imamu remember Mrs. Dawson. "No, man. Her old lady was by the house. . . ." Had it been that day? the day before . . . ?

"I been talking to the old lady, too. She thinks that maybe something done happened to Gladys. Thought maybe you knew. Said you was in the house acting all funny. . . ."

"Yeah, man—I was pretty spaced out. . . ."

"You? What on?" Al Stacy asked.

"Just—spaced out," Imamu said, refusing to deal with last night's scene. "Did she check hospitals?"

"I did. Checked hospitals, precincts, everywhere. I been to her job. She ain't called in. Nobody's seen her. I'm about to blow my stack."

He looked it. On hot days Al Stacy usually looked the coolest man around town. Now, on this cool day, he looked red-eyed and musty—as though he had been through a wringer. It surprised Imamu that the joke about him liking Gladys which they had been kicking around for years had deep roots. "I had hoped you'd help out, man," Al Stacy said.

"Do what I can, Al. But you got to know I spent some nights on the island."

"That is right," Al said. "Forgot . . ." Suspicion that had been showing in his eyes slipped away.

"I'm stopping by to see her old lady," Imamu said. "Whatever I can do . . ."

He joined Olivette, who was waiting a short distance away, and they walked toward his street. "What's that about?" Olivette asked.

"Gladys, she ain't home. Maybe she met a dude she wanted to shack up with," Imamu said. "Stopping by to see her old lady."

"Come on over for dinner?" Olivette asked, when they stopped at Gladys's stoop.

"Not so soon after that gone one yesterday." Imamu

smiled, remembering Flame Larouche's wide green eyes, her smile. Kentucky fries and Big Mac would never be the same. "See you tomorrow?"

"Yes, I'll be there—to finish up," Olivette promised.

"Good. Would be about time," Imamu agreed.

Turning, he saw Mrs. Dawson standing in the doorway. She wore a shawl over the thin-strapped dress she had worn that morning. Her lined face, more lined than Imamu had ever seen it, made her look like a painting. Everybody's mother, he thought as he went up to stand next to her.

"Sorry about this morning, Miss Dawson," he said. "But I was all shook up—something I saw."

"Had anything to do with Gladys?"

"No, ma'am."

"She wasn't in your house?"

"No, ma'am." He shook his head. "I ain't seen Gladys for days." He tried to think back to what day he had seen her. But so much had happened, so much clogging up his mind. He kept shaking his head. "Just days."

"Somebody done something to my gal, Imamu Jones."

"Naw—who would want to do anything to Gladys?" he said. Then thought of Iggy. He kept shaking his head. "Nobody. Gladys ain't a girl that folks mess with."

"She ain't never done this before, Imamu. Gladys don't stay out nights. She be too scared for me."

That's right, he thought, surprised upon remembering. Wild as Gladys was, he had supposed she stayed out whenever she took a notion to—like when she met a dude. But he hadn't known that. "There's always a first time, Miss Dawson."

"She'd call," Mrs. Dawson said. "She'd call me—her job. . . . Gladys might look flighty but she ain't, Imamu.

Least, she responsible to me. Something done happened to her. Something terrible. . . ."

Back on the avenue, Imamu stood on Al Stacy's corner, looking around. He expected Gladys to appear suddenly—fresh and sassy in one of her see-through jobs. Barring that, he hoped Al Stacy would come back and that they could talk about what was to be done. Turning the toothpick between his teeth with his fingers, Imamu wondered about the accident. Someone would have recognized her, if she had been in the wrecked-up car. Someone who might have helped strip her and was afraid or ashamed to say. . . .

Imamu saw Butler walking toward him, unsteady on his feet. He waited until Butler came to the corner, and stood waiting to cross; then he called, "Hey, Butler . . ."

Butler turned, showing signs of a recent fix. But he hadn't forgotten their last meeting. "What you want," he sneered, trying to appear angry.

"Want to know if you seen Gladys."

"Now—what I got to see her for? Got my old lady."

"I ain't asking if you slept with her, man. I just want to know if you seen her around."

"I ain't seen her—not since last night." Butler licked dry lips. He tried to hold himself steady on his feet. "Naw—night before. . . ." He nodded down toward the subway.

"Who was she with?"

Butler shrugged, his eyes closing. He raised his eyebrows high, trying to keep them open. But his knees started bending, down, down. Pulling himself up, he looked around as though already from a long sleep. Then walking from Imamu he stood against the corner building, where he slid to the sidewalk and sat, sleeping.

Imamu stood looking down at Butler. He looked up at the building he was sleeping against. It was the best-kept building on the block. Imamu walked a few steps away and stood looking into the adjoining building. No fire had claimed it. Yet it was as gutted as those next to it, which had been burned out. The ground-floor apartments had opened into each other. Wires, plasters, broken pillars, had fallen or hung around waiting to fall in. Plumbing had been stripped out of the building, like the one next to it. That one had been laid waste by fire. But the water from the pipes from both buildings, which had fallen and dried over the plaster, paint, and all of the leftovers from life, gave out a scent of decay, more rotten than the smell of a swamp or a sewer, more profound than the hot breath of hell, because it breathed the hopelessness of human devastation, of negligence. And it was here that the children of junkies played, here the widows grouped to drink their gut-rotting wines, here the junkies slept when they couldn't make it home or when they had become homeless.

"I been thinking of that too, man." Imamu hadn't heard anyone coming up. Now he turned to find Al Stacy standing behind him, looking into the waste.

For a moment he didn't understand what the man meant. When he did, he said, "Man, you got to be kidding. She can't be in there."

Al Stacy kept staring into the gutted building. "Seen Iggy?" he asked.

"Yesterday—why?"

"He had it in for her. . . ."

"Iggy wouldn't," Imamu said, then wondered why. Why stand up for a stud who had tried to gut him? But Iggy had been on his mind all along. All that change in

Iggy, that new restlessness, on top of his old—had to be about his needing sex—bad.

"Wouldn't he? I was only one half second from doing him in that day, for messing with Gladys. You know that."

"Yeah, but you scared him off, Al."

"That crazy son of a bitch? He don't scare. He just backs off. Know what I mean?"

"I been talking to Butler." Imamu jerked his head toward the sleeper. "Says he seen her couple of nights ago coming from the subway."

"Yeah, checked out on that. She left work that night. Her girls seen her get off at this stop. So she was last seen here, or close to, Imamu."

Iggy, Iggy, Iggy. It didn't seem likely that he'd be into everything. The ring—whatever he had hid in that closet —then have time to mess with Gladys, too. There weren't that many hours for his peanut brain to think up that much evil.

"Oh—he was after her," Al Stacy said. "I ain't seen him the last two days."

"But I did—seen him yesterday."

"Where?"

"His place."

"He's laying low—for a reason."

Imamu forced himself to think back to his last meeting with Iggy. Had he been hiding anything—besides the jewelry hidden in the closet? Imamu closed his eyes, his lips twisting hard around the toothpick. He had been so scared. All he could think up was the look of the knife— he could almost feel his gut being slit.

"Don't know, Al Stacy. Iggy's staying home don't mean—"

"Sticking up for the stud, Youngblood? When you ever know that turkey to just sit at home?"

"Iggy stays home, man. He ain't got no place else to go." Habits die hard. Iggy had looked out for him so many years. . . . "But you got to know, I'd be the hardest one on him, if he messed with Gladys," Imamu added.

"Find out why he's scared to come out," Al Stacy barked, his chin jutting out. "If anyone can get anything outa that crazy son—you can."

Imamu looked at Al Stacy walking off and the hairs on the back of his neck curled. What did a good detective do? Go out and get all the facts. Eliminate the impossible. But detectives usually started out armed with a piece.

Imamu stood over Butler, deciding to wait until he got up. But he hadn't eaten all day. It was late and he was hungry. Could he make it to McDonald's and back before Butler woke? Deciding he couldn't, Imamu walked instead up to the newsstand, bought some pickled pig ears from the gallon jar, and ate them walking back. Still, when he returned, Butler was gone.

Going to his block, Imamu went to Butler's spot, and said to a young stud standing in front of the building, "Hey, man, seen Butler come by?" The stud shook his head. Imamu bent to search through the opening, hoping to see Babs or the kid. He didn't. Going to stand on his stoop, Imamu tried to figure out where Butler might have gone. Anywhere. Straight for a while, high on his fix, he might have decided to act normal and have gone to meet Babs and the kid somewhere, or taken them out. Or he might be trying to find some loot.

Iggy's? Why not? He had found loot there before. He

might think to find some there again. Or find out where
the loot had come from. Dangerous. But addicts lived
damn dangerous lives.

Reluctantly, Imamu left his stoop, heading toward
Iggy's. He walked slowly, not wanting to get there; then
as he went down the block, he breathed in relief as he
saw Butler come out of Iggy's house. Running down the
stoop, Butler headed for the park.

"Hey, Butts," Imamu called. "Got some talk for you."
Butler looked around. Wide awake now, the craftiness
alive in his eyes, he studied Imamu as he came up.

"What you want from me?" he asked. The morning
had indeed decided the status of their friendship. Butler
wasn't having it. "Just want to find out about last night,
man."

"Last night?"

"Yeah, when you seen Gladys."

"She missing or something?"

"Something. . . ."

"Think maybe somebody done her in?"

"Don't know—just asking around."

"Well, it ain't last night I seen her, it was the night
before," Butler said. And it hovered over them the reason he was so definite. He knew what he had done the
night before. Imamu's heart raced. He wanted to walk
away. But he hadn't come to ask about no car accidents.
Then Butler said, "Seen Iggy that night, too."

"Guess lots of folks were out that night, man. Hot.
Streets were humming."

"It was late," Butler said. "Late enough for Gladys to
be from work. She was walking from the subway. . . .
And just after, I seen Iggy—like he was following."
Imamu looked hard into Butler's face. And it occurred to

him that the anger there was recent—as from a few minutes before.

"That Iggy's getting mighty quick with that blade," Imamu took a chance to say.

"Yeah—the crazy mother. . . . They better hurry and put him back where he belongs." He looked back at Iggy's building, then rushed down the block.

Imamu looked back too. Iggy stood on his stoop. And seeing the pointy face, the head with its cap turned backward, he wondered if the smartest thing was to walk up to him, particularly so soon after Butler was hightailing it away. Some detective, he thought. Scared even to question the suspect. Nevertheless, Imamu walked up to Iggy, glad to have him out in the wide open street talking, instead of face to face in his apartment.

"Hey, man, got some talk for you," he said.

Iggy glared at Imamu, then looked away from him. He walked down the stoop, slipped around Imamu, and started down the block. Imamu followed, walking fast to catch up. "Wait up, man. I just wanted to find out if you seen Gladys."

"Ain't none of your damn business, Imamu Jones."

"Seems that her old lady been looking for her, Iggy. Gladys ain't been home."

"I don't give a damn if the broad never gets home," Iggy said and quickened his steps.

Looking at Iggy, Imamu thought of rats—of rats racing ahead to get nowhere. And then he heard that note in Iggy's voice that told him he had heard of Gladys's disappearing. How?

"But you seen her," Imamu said. Iggy kept on walking. Imamu hardened his voice. "Don't walk off from

me, man. I could have ratted on you—and Pierre—
about that job. Instead, I'm the one they put on the
books. But seeing we ain't tight no more." He shrugged
his shoulders, letting Iggy walk on. But Iggy only walked
a short distance before he spun around, then came back
to Imamu.

"What you mean, man?" Iggy called after him. "What
about me and Pierre? What job?"

Instinct. Pure instinct. Imamu knew they had had to
be up to something, the two of them. Pierre's guilty face
had haunted him. Iggy's rabbit run. So he kept on. "That
wasn't your kind of thing, man. You left some tracks—
wide tracks—get what I mean? I known you long enough,
Iggy, to spot any trail that you make. You got to know
that?"

"How you mean, man? How you mean?" But now it
was Imamu who walked away. At least that was giving
off like a detective—one of the wise ones—knowing it all
and never knowing nothing. "Never mind," he said.
"Just remember—you ain't never been able to hide a
thing from me."

"Come on—man. What you talking about?" Iggy kept
trotting to keep up with Imamu.

"What you know about Gladys? Where's she?" Imamu
asked.

"You just talking. You don't know one—not one
damn thing."

Imamu put a toothpick in his mouth and kept on walking. A breeze blowing out his shirt. Had he come on too
strong? Had there been fear in Iggy's voice? Desperation? Imamu ached to turn to read the shifty eyes. But as
long as Iggy was trying to keep up with him, it was Iggy

who had the doubts. So he kept on walking, deliberately
going on to Al Stacy's corner, so that Al could take over
the dirty work.

And the minute Al Stacy saw Imamu, and saw Iggy
trotting behind, he walked up to meet them. "Got something for me?"

"Can't say if I do," Imamu said, jerking his head
toward Iggy. Al went to Iggy, looking into his face.

"Got something to tell me, punk?"

"Me? What I got to say to you?" Iggy said, stepping
away from Al Stacy.

"Where's my lady?"

"What lady?" Iggy sneered. "If you talking about
Gladys, she wasn't no lady."

"What you mean wasn't?" Imamu asked. And Iggy,
seeing his mistake, walked away from them. But Al
Stacy reached out and grabbed him.

"Leave go of me. I got to be going," Iggy said.

"You ain't going nowhere," Al Stacy said. "Not unless
you answer. What you mean—was?" He kept a tight
hold on Iggy's slouching shoulder.

"I ain't said was." Iggy tried to shake off the hands.
"It makes me no difference—she still a bitch."

"This building used to be your hangout," Al Stacy
said, jerking his thumb at the wreck he had been looking
into earlier. "You used to go in and out of there all the
time."

But they used to go in and out of all the buildings—
when the buildings were in better condition. "Man,"
Iggy said, "I just come outa jail. I found that building
like that—what you want from me?"

"You coming in to search it, with me."

"Who? Me?" Iggy jerked out of Al Stacy's hand.

"Make me." He reached for his back pocket. Al Stacy's face went stony, his eyes ugly.

"Anything that comes out of that pocket, you'd better make sure you can digest. Or you've had it."

Iggy's hand froze, dropped away from his pocket. Backing away, he managed to say, "Sh—i—it," then turned and ran. They stood watching as he turned the corner. Then as though the same thought came to them, they looked at each other, and moved toward the building.

14

The support had fallen away from most of the stairway, even the banister. The steps were shaky. And as they went up, the already loose plaster and pieces of concrete rained down on those sleeping on the floor, sending some onto the sidewalk, while others looked up, calling, "Hey, whatcha guys doing up there? You know it ain't safe?"

But it had occurred to Imamu—and he supposed to Al too—that the place, if it had to be searched, had to be done during the daylight. Evening would be impossible, with the lights torn from the walls, and fallen bricks and plaster heaped into mounds all over the floor.

Creaking boards shaking under their weight on the second floor sent more plaster raining down. One girl shouted, "You sons of baboons up there. What you trying to mess with us for? What you all wants? For me to come up there and ram my fist through you. . . ."

Boards ripped up from the floors left openings through which Al and Imamu could look down into the upturned faces, braving it out to be rained down on so they could pile on the abuse.

On the third floor the floorboards held their weight.

Letting in daylight, the broken doors, broken windows, gaping holes in the walls, looked like sockets from which eyes had been torn. And the decay, the mold, rotting wood, let out a funkiness that made Imamu want to vomit.

Leaving the third floor, they walked up to the fourth, where rooms still had doors. Going from room to room, stopping to look into each, a feeling of admiration for Al Stacy grew. Dust had gathered over Al, fallen on his snap-brim hat, made his moustache white. And he didn't seem to care. Nor did he seem to smell the death and decay all around him. His one thought was of Gladys, and he searched with the drive of a man gone mad.

Then they had searched the entire building. The disappointment that overtook them as they came out on the roof to the fresh air kept them both silent. As they looked down the block of adjoining roofs, helplessness overcame them. To go through one building was useless, unless they went through all. And the time it had taken them to go through that one—had brought them into late afternoon.

Going to the front of the roof, Imamu leaned on the restraining wall protecting the roof from the street.

"Look out!" The shout from Al Stacy, as Imamu felt the shifting sheet beneath his hand. He jumped back. Bricks crashed down to the sidewalk. Imamu stood listening. The curses flowed up angrily: "It's them goddamn jackasses up there. They up there trying to kill somebody down here. It better not be me."

Crossing over to the adjoining roof, they started down the steps. Then Imamu remembered that the building had been burned out and had been sealed with tin.

"Maybe these steps don't go all the way," he said.

"We'll just have to go as far as it does," Al said.

It seemed stupid to Imamu to search that building when no one would think of entering it from the outside. Because of the fire, it had to be even more chancy.

But Al Stacy led the way. Imamu followed. The fire had made the wood more fragile. Floors had been burned through. And around the burnt sections, the wood sometimes crunched under their feet or, coming loose, fell in little crashes on the floor below. But the heavy smell of burned wood at least had a cleaner, more healthful smell.

Hugging the walls around the burned-out centers, or scrambling on hands and knees to feel for safety, Imamu remembered Olivette saying: that "they" were punishing black folks for having dared to protest—in the sixties. But he hadn't protested. There had been nothing to protest—and the kids coming after him had had nothing to do with that protest, either. His old man hadn't protested. He had just gone on and served his time in the army—and had died, overseas. So why did Olivette's "they" leave him in a condition like this, and why did "they" leave conditions like this for the babies downstairs?

And Imamu was thinking of the Aimsleys, in their brownstone where he had been sad, and happy, and unhappy—once upon a time—when he heard a crash. Looking up, he saw Al Stacy hanging onto a windowsill, his feet dangling into space. Imamu scrambled on hands and knees and, staying close to the wall, worked his way around the large burned section that took up most of the room. A short distance away from where Al Stacy hung, he worked up to his feet and, still hugging the wall, reached out an arm. Al Stacy grabbed it and steadied himself, by getting a grip outside of the window ledge; then shaking Imamu's hand loose, he climbed up on the sill and sat looking down.

"Damn," he said. "Lost my hat."

Imamu laughed. "Man," he said, "you look like a whiteface minstrel."

Instead of laughing, Al Stacy stared at him from beneath his whitened lashes. "Man, I took you for bright. But you can say some of the damnedest things, at the damnedest kind of times. Do you know how much bread that hat set me back?"

Imamu tried to hold back his laughter. The little man sitting on the windowsill scared to death, yet worrying about a ruined hat, took the day. He kept laughing. Hugging the wall, afraid to take one step back, thinking even as he laughed, this ain't funny. The next step it's likely to be me. Still, he kept laughing. At the sight of Al Stacy on that windowsill, in the white he dug so much, whitened to resemble a plaster cast, beneath his slicked-back, black hair.

And it was his laughing that eased Al Stacy's fear. Shaking his head, Al eased himself down from the window, his feet searching for a strong enough spot to rest. Then grabbing hold of Imamu's outstretched hand, he worked himself next to Imamu, and gingerly, hugging the wall for support, they worked their way out of the room.

But Imamu's laughter seemed to have stirred up something else. "Hear that?" Al Stacy asked, when they were halfway down to the next floor, his hand on Imamu's shoulder holding him still.

"What, man?" Al put up his hand. They stood listening. A quiet lifted between them. A quiet over which they heard the honking of horns from the outside, and the flow of traffic as constant as the tides, slapping against a beach. Imamu hesitated, listening, and through the strange quiet that now enfolded them, he heard a groan. Shivers went down his spine; his hair at the back of his neck bristled. He looked around, expecting to see smoke—white, misty, unreal—moving toward them. How many had been killed in that fire?

Al Stacy backed up the steps. Imamu, wanting to keep close, followed. On the landing, Al moved toward a room they had only glanced in, a small room adjoining the burned-out room where he had almost lost his life. The room had no windows. The only light came from the one they had just left. But they saw it—a bundle, strange, twisted, like clothes heaped in a corner.

They walked slowly toward it, testing the weakened floor. Stepping back as boards threatened to crumble beneath their weight, inching. Wanting to turn back as boards bent, remembering Al's near escape, they got down on hands and knees and crawled. Because of the danger, because it seemed like just a bunch of rags, Imamu wanted to edge back. But there was something compelling about a bundle of rags that had withstood the fire. And suddenly Imamu knew. He had had the feeling before.

His breath came in short gasps of anticipation. His hands slipped in a stickiness. He knew it had to be blood, even before they came to the bundle. And seeing it from close up, the rags were bloodstained.

"Gladys? Gladys . . . ?" Al knelt over the bundle. "Gladys . . ." He moved a bloody rag away. "Baby doll. . . ."

It might have been funny—that name at this time—

except for the pain. Then Imamu recognized the round ball covered in blood as a head—swollen beyond its frame. A face, masked in blood. It was Gladys. Her white slacks, her black halter top. Yes, Gladys. The brick that lay next to her head had a patch of wet curls, wet curly curls stuck to it with blood.

Al Stacy tried to raise her, but her hair stuck to the floor. That swollen head—had it groaned?

"She's alive," Al Stacy said. "She got to be, right? She called out. . . ."

"I better go down and call an ambulance," Imamu whispered.

"You crazy? Those cats would bring down what's left of this building coming up here. It's up to us, man. Grab her legs."

"What if she ain't dead, Al? We might kill her moving her." But Al had already taken out his knife and cut the wet curls keeping her head pinned to the floor. Putting his arm beneath her, he started to lift her. "But, man," Imamu protested. Al cut him off:

"Fool," he said. "If she ain't dead yet, she ain't gonna die. We here to save her—get it?"

He sounded so sure that Imamu took her feet. They carried her, testing every board of the floor as they shuffled toward the door, up to the roof, then over to the next building. And carrying her down the stairs— almost on tiptoe, afraid that what was left of the building might crumble beneath their combined weight—they took her into the street.

Early the next morning Imamu hurried to Harlem Hospital to see Gladys. All night he had been seeing her face and knew that she had died. He thought of her

mother, the unhappy one, who had lost everyone she
ever had to the streets. What was she to do? What could
he do for her? What could anybody do?

But she wasn't dead—yet. Her swollen head swathed
in bandages, breathing through tubes, flanked by bottles
holding liquids that flowed into her arms for nourishment, Gladys lived. "A miracle," the doctor said, when
they had brought her in. "Who can understand the
human will to survive?" And Imamu had wondered,
what if Al Stacy's instincts had not guided him? What if
he hadn't insisted that they search those wrecks of buildings, would her will have held out? How long?

"Takes more than a brick to the head to send you out
of this world, baby doll," Al Stacy said. He was sitting
by the bed, unaware that Imamu had come in. "Hear
what I said, gal," he murmured. "It takes a hell of a lot
more than that to take you outa here—hard as your head
is. You gonna pull out of this—hear me, gal?" Al was a
stud that never showed his feelings—this was as much as
he allowed. It was a lot.

Imamu walked out of the room, into the immaculate
corridor with its starched nurses and intelligent-looking
young doctors, moving around in professional concern.
At the end of the corridor he saw Mrs. Dawson talking
to Otis Brown and McCaully. Seeing Imamu walking
toward her, Mrs. Dawson moved toward him.

"Imamu Jones, who done this? Who done this to my
li'l gal? She's a good gal—all I got in this world. Who
would do such a low thing to her?"

Imamu looked into her suffering, then away, guilty.
Guilty for all those mothers like Mrs. Dawson whose
children had flaked out on drugs, whose dreams for sons

and daughters were flattened out on the tar of the inner city streets, all those who had to tiptoe into their older years with fear as their companion. If he could spare them, he would take all the poisons himself.

"I don't know, Mrs. Dawson," he said. "I don't . . ."

"If you know anything, Jones, this is the time to tell us, man," Otis said, in a friendly voice. "It'll stay between us."

Brown's voice didn't fool him. It only got him angry. Why did they think he had to know—because he had done time, because he had to walk from one place to get to another on the New York City streets? Why did Brown, or anyone else think, that being out there gave him the key to the workings of the slum underworld? The cats in his precinct knew more.

"Man," Imamu said, "if I knew something, I'd dribble out at the mouth. Gladys and me—we grew up together. I just don't know."

"But I do," Al Stacy said, walking up to them. "It's that li'l joker that you punks let out on the streets. Iggy. That's who did this. And, Imamu, you know it."

"I don't." Imamu shook his head.

"You know?" Mrs. Dawson cried. "You know and you ain't gonna tell. And you call Gladys friend. . . ."

"The cat's crazy," Al Stacy said, glaring at the six-footer, Brown. "You known the cat's crazy and you all lets him out. It's you to blame. You all don't give one damn."

"If a man serves his time, he gets out," Brown said, looking all the way down at Al Stacy. "I don't have one thing to do with justice."

"That's right. You ain't," Al Stacy said, ready to take

Brown on. "Just tell me what you got to do with? Putting the squeeze on decent-living, hardworking folks, and letting crooks and pushers go free?"

"Nobody put the squeeze on you—yet—Stacy," Brown said. Then to Imamu: "Where's Iggy, Jones? We been looking for him."

"Ain't he home?" Imamu asked.

"If he was we wouldn't be asking now, would we?" McCaully said. "He's your friend. You and he got busted on that homicide. . . ."

"Whatever you want to know about me is on my disposition sheet, man," Imamu said, and taking a toothpick, put it into his mouth to chew hard on his anger. "If you want to pull me in on charges, now," he said.

"We don't want to do that," Brown said, speaking gently. "We're friends now, ain't we, Jones? You know I'm with you all the way. Got to finish that paint job before your old lady gets home. But you and me got to cooperate." Blackmailing pig. Imamu broke the toothpick with his teeth. That's what being on a policeman's recognizance meant.

"Anyway," Al Stacy said to Mrs. Dawson, "Iggy's got to come out sometime."

"When he does, make sure you get in touch with us," McCaully said.

"I don't get paid to be doing your work," Al Stacy answered.

"Don't get smart," Brown broke in. "You know we can bust you any time we want."

"Do it then, man." Al Stacy spoke softly. "It's got to be cheaper busting me than them studs riding around in them custom-built limos. Them studs so big the only way to miss them is to mix with them."

"Watch out, man," Brown warned.

"Watch what?" Al said, goading him. "You know I got to know that white gold's heavier than silver. . . ." Brown's hand went, automatically, to his inside jacket pocket. Al Stacy jumped back, ready to go for bad. Detective McCaully moved toward him.

"Oh my God," Mrs. Dawson cried out, almost hysterical. "What's all this got to do with my gal laying in there 'bout to die?"

Imamu looked from them, frozen by her words, to the soft-shoed nurses and doctors going in and coming out of Gladys Dawson's room. Here they all were, tied together —pain, passion, and professional concern. . . . Olivette's words sprang to his mind: Everything is everything. . . .

15

After leaving the hospital, Imamu hurried to the subway. He took the train to Brooklyn. Getting away, out of the inner city for two, maybe even three, days. Being free for a change. He had to have it. Leaving the subway, and walking down the tree-lined Brooklyn street, he felt grateful. Grateful for having a foster family that he could come to. Grateful for a room on this street that he could call his. Grateful for the clean smell of green. The skies were heavy with rain clouds. And he hoped it did rain for the time he'd be here.

Running up the steps of the brownstone, he rang the bell. Immediately, it opened. Ann Aimsley stood at the door in her spotless cotton house dress. God, he had forgotten how great she looked, how always so—just right. "Imamu—my dear. Come in, come in."

He entered the foyer, and automatically looked up the stairs that led to the bedrooms—his room, Gail's room. Then he followed her into the spotless living room, with its plastic-covered chairs, its lovely lamps, the television, the stereo. Being in Ann Aimsley's house was almost like being in heaven.

"I hope you came to stay—awhile," she said. "It's not right that you should be alone. . . ."

"I—dropped by," he said. "Just had to see you."

"I'm glad you came," Ann Aimsley said, sitting on the couch, beneath the picture she had given him when he left. It had been painted by one of her ex-roomers. Of the sea, and people being trapped in the surf. Skirting the coffee table, gleaming in the light of day, he went to the window, to look out at the tree in front of the house, the cars parked along the curb.

"I wanted you to be here with me," Ann Aimsley said. "And I didn't see why you wouldn't—seeing that your mother is in the hospital. She is all right?"

"Yes. . . . Doing fine," Imamu said. "Getting stronger and stronger. Be home soon. . . ."

"Then you should stay until she's out."

But he had come to stay. Why didn't he tell her? He looked over at her—her smooth brown face, made rich-looking by the thick gray hair. "Hear from Gail?" he asked.

"I got a card. Didn't you?"

"Haven't been to the post office," Imamu said. "What she have to say?"

"Having a wonderful time—that sort of thing, you know?"

Imamu wondered what Gail had to say to him. He got anxious, suddenly, about the post office. "When's she coming back?"

"Next week. It won't be long before school. . . ."

And so the summer was almost gone. And he had not finished the painting. He stared out the window, brooding. Mrs. Aimsley sat, studying him. "Is everything all right?" she asked.

No, nothing is right, he wanted to say. Everything is wrong. I been to jail, I'm out on bail. I got a friend who's almost dead. . . . And then he thought of Olivette and wanted to see him. Olivette would worry about him. Maybe he had gone up to the house. . . . "Everything's fine," he said. "Just had to see you, though," he said. "Missed you." Why didn't he just tell her he had come to stay?

"Peter will be so glad you've come. He keeps asking about you." The picture of Peter Aimsley, with his strong square face, his broad shoulders, and big workingman's hands, jumped to Imamu's mind. He smiled, liking him, and turned to look into Ann Aimsley's searching eyes—prying eyes. "Are you sure there isn't something you want to tell me, Imamu?"

"Well, I came . . ." She bent over to pick up an invisible something from the carpet. Imamu wanted to run.

He had wanted to be here, with her. But suddenly he didn't want to talk to her—about anything. He didn't want to hear her say: Imamu, I think that's perfectly terrible. Go right home, pack your clothes, and bring them right back here. Peter and I will talk to that Detective Brown.

No, what he wanted, what he always wanted, he knew now, was Gail. She didn't see things in terms of right and wrong. Gail would say: Imamu I'll go with you. If you don't think it wise to talk to Iggy, we'll go to Olivette and together we'll confront Pierre. And of course, that's what he had to do. He walked over to Ann Aimsley.

"Oh now, Imamu, don't tell me you're leaving? You just got here."

"I just had to drop by and give you a kiss." He

grinned and kissed her cheek. "But now I know I got a card waiting at the PO—I got to go."

Leaving the subway when he got uptown, Imamu went over to Iggy's. He rang the bell, not expecting an answer. But talking to Iggy first was doing the right thing. The door opened. Iggy's mother stood there. "Miss Brown," Imamu said, surprised. Mrs. Brown worked hard. She had a sleeping-in job, had had it for years, and only came home on Thursdays. It was Saturday. "I came to talk to Iggy," he said.

"He ain't here," Mrs. Brown said. "He ain't been here all night. The police come—late last night. Woke me out of bed looking for him. Damn fools. What they let him out for? They'd known they'd be after him again."

"He might come back . . ."

"If he does, I'm right here waiting."

To do what, turn him in? Imamu wanted to ask. But he shook his head, following Gail's course. He didn't want to see anything in right and wrong terms. He had never considered Mrs. Brown a "good mother." But what was a good mother—or a good child? That was something he had to think through—when he had more time.

Slowly, thoughtfully, Imamu headed for Olivette's. He looked up at the heavy gray sky. Now, he didn't want it to rain. He wanted it to remain drab, and uncomfortable, but dry. This Iggy business puzzled him. So much against Iggy? Why had he had to fight Gladys out in the streets? Everybody had seen. Everyone had heard his threats to her. But the ring—Butler? Just too much pointed at him —and too little pointed to Pierre—except in Imamu's mind.

Imamu kept his mind on Pierre, his long, thin body,

the long fingers. He thought of the ten dollars he had given him to shop—which had turned to twenty dollars' worth of groceries—and Pierre's innocent, frightened look. He had to talk to Olivette.

But Imamu had to force himself down the block toward the brownstone where the Larouches lived. Iggy was hiding out. Pierre had to know where, and he, Imamu, had to get it out of him. Then what? Did he politely turn Pierre and Iggy over to Brown? Why not? Iggy was a killer. And it might do Pierre good to be stopped now. But who was he to say? Imamu Jones the judge?

Coming to the brownstone, Imamu put his foot on the first step, then stopped. Why did he have to be the one? "They" had had Iggy in jail. "They" knew he was out of his mind. "They" had let him out. Then why should "they" expect him to point the finger? To save himself? Hell, he wasn't guilty—no matter what a barrel full of blond chicks said. Let them prove it. And his mother . . . ?

"Imamu," Flame Larouche smiled as she opened the door. Imamu decided that something real nice had happened to him. Flame had made his day. He followed her up the stairs to the apartment, noticing the way her hips —wide and soft, for so small a woman—shook beneath the green-and-gold striped dressing gown.

And when they entered the apartment and she sat with her feet curled beneath her on the couch, her shining red hair framing her face, her eyes flirting, he decided that the most wonderful thing that had been done him, in days, was to be admitted to her parlor.

Looking at her from the chair he was sitting in, Imamu felt himself stretching out of it, his shoulders broadening. Nothing in the world was as bad as it seemed. The lovely woman, that most gorgeous of women, thought that he was handsome—very, very handsome. It had been so long since he had thought of himself that way that the question he asked seemed more than a little stupid:

"Know where Olivette is?"

"No—I thought he was with you. . . ."

Imamu sat hesitating, knowing he should leave, go out and find Olivette. But Flame Larouche kept looking at him, looking him over. And then she moved over on the couch and patted the seat next to her. "I had hoped to see you—last night. . . ."

"Lots of things"—he stared—"been keeping me busy."

"Olivette's been telling me—about the painting. He's been helping you. I'm glad. Olivette so rarely has friends that he cares so much for. I wanted to know you better."

A flush of pleasure burned to Imamu's face, confusing him. He didn't know whether it was because of this lovely woman, who seemed to want his company—or because Olivette had been praising him to his mother. "I always wondered what somebody Olivette really cared for would be like," Flame Larouche said. "It's awful that you both had to get in this—terrible situation for me to get to meet one."

"But I supposed Olivette makes friends easy," Imamu said. "He likes people so very much." Then as Mrs. Larouche's eyes widened in surprise, he rushed to add, "He understands about people."

"Does he?" she said skeptically. Then she added, "You mean he's brilliant—yes, that he is. . . ."

"You all are such a fine family," Imamu said. "So

—so good to look at—fine. . . . Know what I mean?"

"You think so?" She looked up at him as though she agreed. Then lowered her lashes, coquettishly, making her appear, very young, very shy.

"Your—your husband must have been very proud—of all of you," Imamu said.

"But I have never been married." Flame Larouche looked at him, surprised. And Imamu realized that he was snooping, trying to find out things that Olivette had not told. He had never mentioned his father. But Flame Larouche didn't seem to mind. Stretching her arms over her head, she leaned her head back so that the smooth skin of her fair neck became unbearably touchable. She glanced at him from the corner of her eye. "No, the boys never had fathers—that they know—nor for that matter did I. . . ."

"Oh. . . ." The simple way she admitted these things embarrassed Imamu.

"But I had a lovely mother, gorgeous—even if she was a bitch. . . ." Flame grunted in satisfaction, then laughed. "Her grandmother was a slave."

Imamu looked at her, trying to think back to what he knew about his grandmother or great-grandmother. Nothing. Sure, most black folks knew there was slavery all mixed up in their backgrounds—that's what it was all about. But no one kept up with who, when, where.

Flame jumped up and, going to the unused fireplace, took an album that was lying on the mantel. She came back to the couch, and sat next to Imamu, touching him. The smell of her perfume rushed to Imamu's head, along with his blood. He eased out his breathing, trying to appear calm.

"Here she is," Flame Larouche pointed with pride at the picture of a very severe, very black, withered woman in a high-collared black dress, staring out of the page at them.

"She lived to be old—very old. Outlived her master by at least fifty years. She was over one hundred and ten when she died. Her master treated her—and his children —quite well. We all still bear his name. . . ." She turned the page. "This is great-grandfather," she said, about the slight-looking, almost girlish-looking young white man, with a moustache. . . . Then she turned the page. "This is their daughter. My mother's mother. Her name was Flame."

The picture might have been one of the woman beside him except that it was of another time—with girdled waistlines and full bosoms in style. Her half-exposed bosom blossomed out over a low-cut neckline. "She was very beautiful," Flame Larouche said with a laugh, as though complimenting herself. "And exceedingly wealthy. Her father saw to that. . . . The Louisiana French, you know."

The next picture was that of an obviously grand lady. She had black hair styled high on her head. "Grandmother. . . ." Mrs. Larouche said, of the dark-eyed woman with a haughty face. "Grandmother was courted by royalty. So it's safe to say that mother was of royal blood." She laughed, a bitter laugh—turning the page. "She—believed it."

This woman was beautiful without the haughtiness of the others. In a simple dress, hair parted in the center, two long braids, hanging to her shoulders. She looked out calmly, almost sadly from the page. "God, that woman was selfish—spoiled. She went through all grandmother's money. Left us without a dime."

Flame Larouche breathed angrily, then with an effort, calmed herself. "So, you see—we, none of us, are of the marrying breed."

Imamu had never heard of a nonmarrying breed, had in fact always accepted that living together unmarried was a sin. Just like going to bed without being married had a sinful quality—which made the need more exciting—but still a sin. And now, to hear that all these real gone women—mulattoes who by the look of them could have had their choice in men—had spent their lives single, rich, satisfied to go along under the old master's name. . . . That blew Imamu's mind.

"Does that have anything to do with Olivette not going into the seminary?" he asked, stabbing in the dark.

"So he told you about that, did he?"

"I—I. . . . Wasn't he supposed to?"

"Who cares." She shrugged her shoulders. "You have no idea how I worked, the strings I pulled—all to get him that scholarship. . . . And then he goes and gets ideas. . . . What difference if he becomes a priest; he isn't going to marry—or have children. Not that it matters. . . ."

"I broke the pattern, when I had boys," she said crossly. "It's the end of a breed. Mother put an end to the money. I put an end to the breed. And Olivette." She shrugged again. "Can you imagine anyone being perfect enough . . . ?" Her eyebrows raised, her eyes flashed angrily, then she added, "Do you think the girl has yet been born, dear Imamu?"

"There can be grandchildren," Imamu said. Flame Larouche shrugged.

"A woman's child is always her own, Imamu. It doesn't matter who's the father—or grandmother."

Strange family. Imamu kept thinking of them as he walked down the avenue. There were so many things Flame Larouche had left unsaid. It was like talking in code, leaving much to be filled in. He had wanted to question her, talk more and more. Thoughts about their lives had come to him, only to be silenced in the air, to sit on his lips, or poised at the edge of his mind, to melt like jellyfish exposed to the sun. Because—and Imamu knew this—she had chosen just what she wanted him to know.

Deep in thought, he walked, until someone fell in step with him. Olivette. He knew without looking. Then they walked together, silently, crossing the street. They walked toward Imamu's house, and Imamu knew that the inevitable time had arrived. Why not? What the hell would they do with the rest of the day, if not finish painting his house?

"How is Gladys?" Olivette said, breaking the silence.

"Bad," he said. And as they walked on: "It's not to be believed how a woman can get beaten like that—and live."

"So, she's going to make it?"

"The doctors don't know—but Al Stacy says she will. Says Gladys's head's too hard for her to go that way. But it sure took a pounding."

"They can keep people alive, almost forever, in the comatose state," Olivette said. "Life-supporting devices, you know. But the brain, once damaged—will never be the same."

"Comatose?" Imamu said. "I don't know. Guess they

have to wait and see. But God, let's hope she lives."

They walked on and for some reason Imamu didn't want to tell Olivette that he had been with his mother. Instead he said, "Where's Pierre?"

"Home—I think."

Then he's got to be with Iggy, Imamu thought. He glanced at Olivette's serious profile. This was as good a time as any to tell him about Iggy, about Pierre, his suspicions. But they could talk while they were working. Still, Imamu felt a strain developing between them. Or maybe it was only in him. Whatever happened, he had no intention of doing time. Not even if catching Iggy meant putting the finger on Pierre, too. He thought of Flame—the beautiful Flame. And he thought of Olivette's coming to him, thinking only of helping him finish the perfect paint job.

"Hey, Imamu," Babs called as they walked by her. She sat on a slab of concrete, in front of the bombed-out building. Her kid was sleeping in her arms. "D'you hear? They picked up Butler, last night."

"No jive? What for? Possession?"

"Breaking and entering. But he ain't had nothing to do with that—or beating on that white man," she said. "He got that stuff from that simple-brain, Iggy."

So, that's why they were looking for Iggy. They had been after Iggy for that job. It was sure, if Butler was going cold turkey, he'd open up and scream like a baby. Tell just where he got the stuff. And now Gladys—they were trying to tie the two together. "Yeah, that Iggy goes for crazy. But even a crazy fool like him ought to know better than to go around beating on rich white folks' head. There ain't no win. And there sure ain't no win for him if they trying to jail my old man. . . ."

16

So, in the minds of the police, the Phantom Burglar had been narrowed down to Iggy. But Imamu knew that if Iggy had something to do with it, so had Pierre. Iggy was a bad dude, crazy bad, not slick bad. Giving pain, and getting satisfaction from it, was more his thing. But Pierre . . . ? Imamu frowned, thinking: The tenseness that Olivette had shown when he thought Pierre had disobeyed him—that was fear. And Mrs. Larouche, going into her mother-act over Pierre—overprotecting him—wasn't that fear, too? Imamu kept thinking of the ten-dollar bill he had given to Pierre at their first meeting. Olivette might have worked overtime trying to push perfection into Pierre, but Pierre was no genius. He was just another ordinary kid—out there, in the street.

They painted the hallway quickly, each taking one side. While they worked, Imamu heard Olivette talking without Imamu's once hearing what he said. They were almost finished when it struck Imamu that Olivette was talking as abstractedly as he had been listening. He stopped work to turn to Olivette. The time had come to discuss what was uppermost in both their minds. Olivette stopped work too. He looked through the bedroom to the window.

"Have you noticed that the days are getting shorter?" he said. "It's just after seven and already it's almost dark.

"The weather," Imamu said. "It's going to rain." It was also near enough to the end of August to worry about September trotting in. "Soon our case will be coming up, Olivette. If they don't know who's been into that mess—they'll pin it on us sure."

"Imamu, is that's what's worrying you?" Olivette asked. "I thought you were being pleased because we were finishing up this job at last." He laughed triumphantly. "Your mother will be home to a delightful new house."

It was because they had finally finished that Imamu went to see his mother before going to see Gladys, the next day. But he regretted that as he entered her room. He had nothing to say. He couldn't tell her about her surprise. And besides, his mind was on other things.

"What's the matter, son?" she asked when he had been there only a few minutes. "What you done now?" That hurt him.

"You sure got a lot of faith in me," he said jokingly.

"Faith . . . ? You a good boy," she said. "But I know things be happening out there."

They sure had. Her understanding that things might happen to him over which he had no control touched him. He took her hands and kissed them. "I lay in here thinking," she said. "Ain't many sons would come all this way to see a simple ol' lady who ain't got enough sense to stay away from the bottle."

"You ain't old and you ain't simple," Imamu said.

"And you know enough now so you won't be nursing no more bottles." He brushed back her hair and wished she hadn't become gray, and that her eyes were not so faded, so ready to receive worry.

Uptown, he decided that instead of going to see Gladys he'd go to Olivette's and finish out the talk he hadn't been able to get started. But turning down their street he saw Brown's car parked in front of the brownstone.

And when Imamu rang the Larouche bell, Otis Brown came down to open the door. "I been looking all over for you," the big man said. Imamu stood looking at Brown, wanting to turn away. It was sure Olivette and Pierre were out, for Brown to open the door.

"Come on in," Brown said. "You got things you got to tell me, right?" Imamu stood hesitating. "Look, man," Brown said. "I'm the one helped bail you out, remember? I got my reputation on the line because of you."

Because of Flame Larouche, Imamu wanted to say. But what difference? If Olivette hadn't pressured his mother to pressure Brown . . . ? It had been Brown who had done it. He walked in.

Going up the stairs, he asked, "What you want from me, Brown?"

"Only want to know what you know."

"About what?"

"About where Iggy's holed up."

"That, I don't know."

"Jones, you got to know. That stud ain't for real. Why you still trying to protect him? We gonna get him and I bet he don't protect you."

"Why you want to talk like that to me, man?" Imamu said. He had come to the apartment and stopped at the door as the smell of perfume hit his nose. It forced him to remember Flame Larouche the way he had last seen her, even before he looked into the room to see her stretched out on the couch, in a sheer gown. His eyes went over her body, even while trying not to; then he turned from her with a jerk. Brown was dressed in his usual brown and yellow. His scrubbed face, fresh-looking and shouting out all about love, stood between him and the door.

"If I tell you I don't know anything at all, Brown, haven't known one damn thing, would you believe me?" Imamu asked.

"No."

"Then I better not tell you," Imamu said.

"A li'l bit of loot, is worth the life of your friend?" Brown asked.

"Loot? What loot?"

"From the Phantom Burglaries. . . ."

"Come again?"

"We got your friend Butler. He's been dribbling at the mouth."

"Brownsie." Mrs. Larouche stretched out a helpless hand to the big man. "Stop bothering my guest with police work."

"Flame, you don't understand. This character is buddy to that lunatic."

"You got that wrong, Brown," Imamu said. "We ain't been buddies since—" Imamu checked himself before he said since Pierre and Olivette had been around. He had planned to. He wanted to get the mess straight. But suddenly he knew he couldn't, might never be able to. Instead, he said, "Since he come out. He stays away from me. He knows I'm straight."

"Folks seen him with you."

"What folks? Butler?"

"Among others."

"That junkie would say whatever you want him to say. I know you got him."

"He saw you going into Iggy's house. Deny that."

Imamu checked his anger, trying to remind himself that, by some miracle, called Flame Larouche, the turkey had found a soft spot in Brown's brain to help him. "Man, I know lots of folks what lives in Iggy's house. So just because he's out, I can't go see them?"

"Come on. Iggy's been your number one man."

"Brownsie," the lady pouted. "Imamu's been close to Olivette, not to anybody else." She crossed two dainty fingers, kissing them. Brown went to her taking her hands, the soft spot in his brain showing.

"Baby, the dudes from around these streets ain't half as innocent as they make out. Believe me, I know. That Iggy is a natural killer. He's out there and somebody got to know where he is. And let me tell you, that somebody is right here." But he let Flame pull him down beside her.

Imamu sat in a chair opposite, looking at them. He dug seeing them together. The big man. The sexy lady with her dainty feet and hands. But as he sat looking at their scene, the thought occurred that Brown had been thinking the same way he had. Iggy had to have someone with him for the burglaries. He didn't have the kind of mind to go it alone. What Brown didn't know, and what Imamu didn't tell him, was that Iggy was a solid block boy. A lonely one. He had to be hiding out somewhere around the block. If somebody wasn't in constant touch with him, Iggy most likely would have walked out and have already been in his hands.

Without consciously making a decision, Imamu stood
up and stretched. He had to get on the avenue, look
things over, think things out.

"You got to know you're wrong, Brown," he said. "If
I had still been friends with the dude, do you think I'd
have let you bail me out?"

Imamu didn't see that one had to do with the other.
Chances are neither did Brown.

Before Brown could challenge Imamu on that, the
doorknob rattled, the door flew open, and Pierre rushed
in. "Imamu, Iggy wants . . ." Pierre looked at Brown and
his big eyes grew bigger. He caught his hands, the fingers
twisting into each other. He stood biting his lip, staring
at Brown. But Brown seemed to have suddenly seen
something to mar the shine of his shoes. He looked down
at them, then bent and got to brushing them. Imamu kept
staring at Brown, who didn't look up. So Imamu walked
out.

17

Discord. The jarring of his insides. His mind stretching in different directions—like listening to different tunes, different types of music, symphony, jazz, being played from different parts of the same room—pulling his mind, here, there, keeping him unfocused.

Rain had begun to fall as Imamu headed up the block. Big drops hit at his head, the back of his neck, his chest. Along the sidewalks folks looked skyward, not daring to believe that, at last, the rain was actually falling. Imamu expected a downpour. Yet he drifted up the avenue, determined to hold on to the impression that kept filtering over, instead of into, his mind. His feet turned toward the park, where walking slowly up the steps, jostling folks heading for drier places, he climbed over the iron rail and made his way through the patches of mangy weeds, to the big boulder.

Sitting beneath it, looking down toward the avenue, Imamu tried to jolt his mind. What was disturbing him? He retraced his steps, from the time he had left the subway that afternoon. He saw himself standing at the door of Harlem Hospital, then walking to the Larouche home.

He thought of Brown opening the door, of his trip upstairs behind the big man. In the apartment he let his
mind go around the room with the drapes, which when
closed made the place into two rooms. . . .

The drops of rain had stopped. But the clouds hung
low and heavy, promising that they had only given a
sample. Steam rose from the musty sidewalks, and shim-
mered in the air. A smell of green, loosened by the rain,
misted with the smell of the suddenly dampened earth.

Imamu opened his shirt to air his chest in the stifling
humidity. He thought of Flame—her heavy perfume and
her dainty hands, the way they flayed the air, helpless.
He thought of Brown, big, masterful, sitting at her side
staring at his shoes.

Someone waving caught his attention. Olivette. He
waved back. And as Olivette walked up the hill toward
him, the swing of his shoulders, his strong-looking neck,
sent a thrill of pleasure through Imamu. A handsome
dude. Olivette came up with his I-like-you smile.
"Mother said you had been to the house," he said. "I
tried to catch you—went by your place. . . ."

"Decided I needed air," Imamu said. "I waited at
your place, but Brown gave me a hard time. I needed
some space."

"Oh? Was Brown there?"

"Was when I left," Imamu said. "Looking like he was
trying to decide if he wanted to shine his shining shoes."

Olivette laughed, delighted. "I often wonder in which
Brown takes the most pride—his shoes or his car. They
both have the same quality of preciousness, you know."

"Brown takes pride in shining his car, in shining his
shoes, and in putting shines in studs' eyes, when he gets
them in the precinct," Imamu said.

Olivette laughed again. "You exaggerate about Brown," he said. "He really is a lovely man. . . ."

A sudden downpour prevented Olivette from going on to say more about the great influence Brown was having on him. For a few seconds they looked at each other, waiting for the move to run. But Imamu leaned back, letting the water beat down on his chest, and Olivette sat beside him, leaning back, too. The heavy rain soaking them forced Imamu to concentrate on the unaccustomed wetness of his jeans, his soaking underwear, for a time. Then he said, "Your mother is quite a lady. I liked talking to her."

"About?"

"Everything in general."

"That covers quite a lot." Olivette closed his eyes to let the rain wash over his face.

"She showed me your family album. You all sure got some history, man. I mean—you all know about it."

"You saw the picture of grandmother, of course."

"Beautiful lady."

"Yes. An aristocrat. Wealthy. But then money had come down through the family from great-great-grandfather, you know." Olivette turned up his mouth and, through the falling rain, Imamu didn't know if in pleasure or distaste. "I suppose you saw his picture, too. Mother has great fantasies about the patriarch."

"She seemed to have a lot more pride in your great-great-grandmother, the slave."

"Ah—if it was so. That's Mother's way of getting back at Grandmother, who hated black people. Mother blamed her for our being poor.

"You see, Grandmother was extravagant. She never cared about money. She never had to. Money had always been a part of her life. Then the Depression—that caused all her losses, really. She didn't have any understanding about finances—no more than Mother. But she had spoiled Mother so much. . . ."

"You knew your grandmother?"

"Yes. I adored her. She made life so good for us. I was eight when she died. But Mother. . . . She decided that since Grandmother had left us paupers, we would live like paupers . . . like poor blacks, in other words. It was her way of getting even. . . ."

"Did you know anything about poor people before?" Imamu asked.

"You mean, poor black people," Olivette corrected him. "No, Louisiana mulattoes—consider themselves a pretty special group. Even the poor ones. I had never even thought of myself as being black, until I—we became poor. I doubt if Mother ever had. . . ."

Imamu fumbled to open up the pocket of his wet shirt. He needed a toothpick to help his mind to focus, to deal with what he was hearing. But before he could get one out of the pocket, Olivette had changed the subject of their conversation. Looking around the park, he said, "I love parks in New York. Parks everywhere are nice. But in New York they're special. Parks, you see, were built with one aim—to afford a leisure class lovely surroundings. But in New York the poor defied that kind of logic —didn't they? They kept creeping closer, and closer— until now they are at the edges of every park in the city." He let the rain beat down on his closed eyes for a minute, giving to his face a ghostlike, almost angelic quality.

Imamu checked an urge to reach out and wipe away the water, to keep wiping away the water so long as it fell upon the face of his friend. Was Olivette real? Flame

Larouche—all those who had come before—that breed
of people, the fair, beautiful mulattoes, whose breed
could become extinct because of the birth of sons—were
they real? Had he stumbled onto a fragment of history—
black history—a dark, secret corner of the country into
which he had been allowed a peek? Was any of it real?
Was it real for him to be sitting here, in this hard-hitting
rain, looking at the lovely face of this boy genius, a boy
who had decided to be his friend—a friend whom he
found it so hard to reach out to, even to touch . . . ?

Olivette opened his eyes, and for a moment they
looked through the rain at each other. Words crowded
Imamu's mind, fell to his mouth. But before they could
be formed into a meaningful sentence, sirens sounded
from the avenue, jolting him back to the moment. "Did
you say Brown wasn't there when you got home?" he
asked, suddenly apprehensive.

"No—he wasn't."

"And Pierre—was he there?"

"No."

Jumping to his feet, Imamu started down the hill, running. He leaped over the iron railing, ran out of the park,
dashed across the avenue, slouching in water, ankle-deep
in the street. He ran to Eighth Avenue. At the corner he
saw the patrol cars, emergency vans, jamming the avenue. Policemen formed a cordon to keep a pushing,
shouting crowd back. Ducking beneath the restraining
arm of a policeman, Imamu gained the avenue, ran almost the length of the block before he was caught and
herded back behind the cordon.

All the activity was going on around the abandoned
house, next to the one in which he and Al Stacy had
found Gladys.

And where a moment before everything seemed unreal, the policemen, the sounds of the sirens, the yelling
crowd, suddenly there was a frightening reality. Because
Imamu saw Detective Brown coming out of the building
carrying a bullhorn. Stepping out into the street, Brown
looked up to the higher floors. He shouted through the
horn: "Come on, Iggy. Come down now. You don't have
a chance."

Standing at the edge of the crowd, Imamu looked back
searching and immediately saw Pierre. His first instinct
was to go to him. But Olivette, who had run from the
park with Imamu, was already with his brother. Imamu
saw Al Stacy standing a short distance from him. "Hey
Al," he waved. "What's happening, man?" Al worked his
way close to Imamu.

"They gonna get that sucker," he said between closed
teeth. "Damn shame. They gonna get him before I can
get my hands on him." But another voice, behind them
—a woman's voice—cried out: "Pray, pray that he give
hisself up. They ain't got no right in the world to be
hunting down a poor boy like that. All them grown
mens? All them guns?" Imamu found comfort that she
was there, in that crowd. And he found himself praying
with her, for Iggy.

All those cars? All those guns? But they didn't know!
They had no proof that Iggy had been the one who had
beaten the man Auerbach, or that he had beaten in poor
Gladys's head. They didn't really know that he was in on
the Phantom Burglaries. But it didn't matter. It didn't
matter any more than it had when they had pulled him in
for carrying a shopping bag, or when they had pulled him
and Olivette in for walking the streets. They had been
given the go-ahead on the Iggys, the trapped ones of the

ghetto long, long ago. It didn't matter and everyone knew it didn't matter.

"Give yourself up, boy," the woman behind him moaned. "Go on, honey—give up. . . ."

But Iggy, the trapped one, had as much chance of giving up as the restless geni in his body had of lying down to die. No. Iggy had to have it out. He didn't believe in his chances. Good reason. Iggy never had had chances. And he knew it. Wasn't that what was so frightening about him? Wasn't that why he, Imamu, had tried to keep his distance from him? Because Iggy had never had a chance?

Tears rose to Imamu's eyes, seeing the big, broad-shouldered policemen in their wet slickers stomping the fragile building. Through the falling rain Imamu could see the loose debris raining down into the cave from their weight. He had to stop his feet from taking out after them, from trying to reach Iggy before they did. *Try to give up, Iggy. Try hard to give up. You got a friend out here. You got friends. . . .*

"They gonna kill him sure," the woman behind Imamu moaned. "They gonna kill him. . . ."

But Al Stacy at his side kept muttering, "All them days—all them goddamn days, he leave the girl up there. . . . Well it's his ass now. . . ."

The tears started down Imamu's face. He thought of the time Iggy had needed him. Iggy had nestled to him for friendship. And even in his twisted mind Iggy had been loyal to him. He hadn't let Imamu Jones take a rap for something that he had done. *You ain't alone, Iggy. It ain't right that you up there alone. . . .* And all through his prayers, the prayers of the woman behind him, Imamu was aware of Olivette standing some distance

away, his hand on Pierre's shoulder. And without looking at Pierre, he saw the boys' hands twisting together.

"There he be," a woman in the crowd shouted. A hush
spread as every head bent back looking, looking up at
Iggy, on the roof, looking down. Looking down at all
those patrol cars, all those police vans, all those policemen—and at Brown with his bullhorn. How was Iggy
supposed to see him, Imamu, in that crowd? How was he
to know that here and there in the press of people looking on for excitement, there were those pulling for him?
Praying for him? Trapped—inside himself as well as
outside—how did he know about prayers and praying?
No one had ever thought about prayers to teach him, or
to pray for him before.

And Imamu, trapped at his side, up there, felt Iggy's
heart beating; he felt the restlessness straining the tense
little body, driving, driving.

The rain must have muted the sounds of the cops on
the steps, so that Iggy could not have heard them. Because suddenly there they were, with drawn guns. Iggy
spun around, leaning back against the restraining wall of
the roof. Imamu heard the explosion of bricks at the same
time he heard someone shout "Look out!" Cops scrambled from the stoop. Bricks came tumbling, tumbling,
hitting the sidewalk with thudding sounds—then a slap
—which created a silence. And in the silence, heads lowered to look at the body that had fallen and lay on the
sidewalk among the bricks.

For moments no one moved. Then one cop moved a
brick from the body with his foot. The crowd surged
forward.

"I declare I ain't never seen nobody more marked for

death in my life," the woman behind him moaned. "Poor boy. Poor, poor boy. . . ."

Al Stacy muttered, "All things considered, he got off too damn easy. . . ."

"Imamu." Olivette had come to where Imamu stood. He put an arm around Imamu's shoulders. "Please, don't cry, Imamu. It wasn't as though Iggy had any kind of future . . ."

Imamu hadn't known he was crying. "Olivette," he said, feeling a pain as deep as he was deep inside. "He was twisted, I know that. But he did need help."

"But you couldn't have helped him, Imamu. He was already lost."

"How do you know that?" Imamu cried. "Who are you to judge. . . ."

"But didn't you judge him, Imamu—when you rejected him . . . ? Now he's no longer a threat—against you—or the neighborhood. . . ."

18

The nip on his ear sent him scurrying, shoving, pushing, forcing his way through—away from the attack, away from the hovering shadow, standing behind them blocking the path to retreat. But he was moving toward the light! He tried to resist his forward thrust. Tried to move back. But hot bodies from behind kept forcing him on. Fur brushed fur, sweat oozed into sweat, sweeping him before them. But he knew the danger: he had intelligence! That escape hatch carried him to his doom—carried them all to destruction!

Digging his claws into the wood of the floor, he fought against those furry bodies, sweeping him on. But they were in the hundreds, the thousands, surging, pushing. In despair he cried out, "Squeak! Squeak!" But the echoing voices, from the hundreds of thousands of rats, responded, "Squeak, squeak, squeak," and they came surging on.

Desperate, he stood on his hind legs to warn them. He prayed, begged, beseeched them. The shadow from behind reaching out, over the rest, ripped into him. He heard the tearing of his skin. The others stopped, sniffing.

Then they turned on him, teeth bared. He shrank into himself, knowing his blood was spurting. They leaped. Claws scratched into him, fangs tore at him. He screeched. . . .

Jumping out of sleep, heart pounding, Imamu sat up reaching for the light. Switching the room into life, he jumped out of bed and walked down the hall, turning on all the lights in the apartment. But the reality of his nightmare remained.

Back in his room, Imamu stood before the mirror. But the nightmare blocked his vision. What he saw in the mirror were the hundreds, the thousands, of scurrying bodies, leaping at him. He sat on the bed, and folding his arms around his knees, he laid his head on them, forcing himself to relive his nightmare.

The sense of being pushed, of being manipulated, filled him. Once again he felt the overpowering helplessness of being locked in, the uselessness of courage, when pitted against the flow of the tide.

And as he sat there, his calm returned, his heart slowed down to its normal beat. And in the quiet that filled him, the confusion of having been pulled apart, of being completely destroyed, disappeared. He knew! God, how simple. So simple. And so logical . . .

Immediately, Imamu pulled on his shirt and jeans. He had to have it out before clear knowledge seeped once again into confusion and self-doubt. Why? He knew what had happened. What he didn't know was how the pieces connected. And he had to know the whole.

Three in the morning. Going to someone's house at that time made no sense. But he couldn't wait. Anyhow, why did he have to make more sense than the turned-about life of the street where he lived—the addicts, the kids out at this time? Weaving his way through the traffic of people, Imamu crossed the street, walking up to the building where Iggy had fallen to his death. He stood there for several minutes, staring at the darkened blood, then had to push himself away. He had to be clear-headed. The ingredients of a good investigative mind had to prevail. No sentiments. None, none, none.

He turned down the street, walked quickly to the middle of the block, ran up the steps of the brownstone, and rang the bell—two long, two short. He knew that the sound throughout the house might bring a mixture of curses and outright physical abuse. Nevertheless, he pushed again. And was surprised when he saw someone coming down the stairs so promptly. The door opened, and he stood face to face with Olivette.

"Imamu? What's happened . . . ?" Olivette searched through Imamu's eyes. Imamu managed to give him an eye-to-eye. "Come upstairs," Olivette said quietly. "I'm watching television—waiting for Mother. She and Brown went out—to dinner. I worry when she stays out too late. . . ."

Concern. Sadness. The benevolent smile, and Imamu knew that the reasons for his own fears were real. In the room—that part left for entertaining when the curtain closed out the other half—the half where Pierre lay sleeping—Imamu stood studying the books on the bookshelf, preparing himself not to be influenced by Olivette's gentle face, his polite manner.

"Come on, Imamu," Olivette said, after waiting for him to speak. "You didn't come this time of the night to borrow books. Something has happened. Your mother? Gladys? Is she dead, Imamu . . . ?"

"You did it, Olivette," Imamu said.

"Then she is dead." Olivette's calm raised doubts in Imamu. Was he still asleep? Was this just a change of scene?

"You did it, Olivette," Imamu repeated. "You killed her." He hadn't come to lie—wouldn't have. But the occasion—Olivette's calm—presented itself. "Why, Olivette? What could Gladys have done that wrong?"

Imamu wanted to turn to see Olivette's face. Fearing that looking into Olivette's face might change his determination, he kept his head bent over the books. The room grew still. The quiet fell heavily to his shoulders. He sensed a stiffening in Olivette. He wondered if he turned to see his anger, or surprise, whether that might influence him. Had the pious, priestly curtain raised to show the out-and-out street cat that lay beneath? The silence kept growing heavy—too heavy. Sadness trembled through Imamu, reaching up to strangle him—a sadness that, had he waited, might have prevented him from seeing this through.

Imamu fought to breathe normally, to appear relaxed. But the muscles of his back stretched, expecting anything, even violence—a fist in the small of his back, a stranglehold around his neck. But only silence, growing, growing, stretching out the walls of the room, pushing, pushing, crumbling the walls, shattering windowpanes, carrying them out into space so that they both floated out there, around each other, sparing. . . .

"She was very aggressive, you know," Olivette finally said in the same tone he had always used. "So—so vulgar . . ."

Imamu spun around. "Because she tried to make you? Man . . ."

"That—and other things."

"Like what, man? What could she have done to have you do her that bad?"

"Imamu—she never let me alone! She studied my every move—knew when I went and when I came. You have no idea . . ."

"You mean that she got a line on your breaking and entering and hit you with it?" Imamu asked, surprised he had said it. Because that part of it he hadn't yet thought out.

"That, too. She was either looking out of the window, or waiting on the stoop when I got back. Then she said to me, 'I got your line and I'm hauling myself into it.' Blackmail—so that I would look at her and love her! Imamu, I tried to ignore her. She just wouldn't have it. She even accused me of setting up your arrest. God, anything that came into that girl's mind, she said. You know I'd never hurt you. . . .

"At that, Gladys was more intelligent than I supposed —connecting me with those burglaries—right off. Then one day, she pretended to be—feeling—my chest and found a watch—an exquisite piece. . . . 'Nobody got to know about this,' she said. . . ."

"And so you beat her to death. . . ."

"I hadn't intended to of course. I had only intended to frighten her—to show her what I was actually capable of. But she wasn't impressed. She wanted to make love. . . . When I didn't—Imamu, you never heard such words —the abuse! Me. Mother. . . . I really couldn't take it, you know."

Imamu knew. He knew Gladys, her bad mouth, her real hatred of being put down. But he knew Olivette, too. He knew his anger. In the weeks they had come to know each other, Imamu had never seen him angry. But he had known—and had been afraid of the anger he had sensed lurking. It had been, after all, so obvious. It had forced him, Imamu, to toe a careful line. He had seen it in Pierre's fear of his brother, in Flame Larouche's defiance of her son.

"And that guy, Auerbach?"

"That was an accident. He came back, you know. He had forgotten something. He caught me. I would have simply walked out—apologized even. But no. 'What are you doing in here, you dirty nigger,' he said to me. I went wild. Then I did try to kill him. But Gladys—no. I had no intention of killing her. I just wasn't able to stop. . . ."

"She isn't dead," Imamu said.

"What! You lied—to me?" His indignation seemed more because of Imamu's lying, than the fact that Gladys still lived.

"Naw, she ain't dead," Imamu repeated. "Hard as that gal's head is. . . ." He used Al Stacy's exact words.

"She's conscious then? You talked to her? Did she tell the police?"

"Don't know, man."

"Then how?"

"Because of Iggy—the way you set him up. I think it came to me as I saw him falling off that roof. . . ."

"I did use Iggy—in a way. . . . I never did anything but let him walk by a house I intended to burglarize. You know—the black walking by to hold everyone's attention. . . ." He laughed. "It always works. Iggy got into trouble because he wanted to be guilty. He and Pierre went back to rob a building I had worked on—that was why we two would-be detectives happened to be pointed out. . . . We all look alike, you know." Olivette laughed again. "Another accident. But the worse was losing control of Iggy."

"What made you think that Iggy would stand for it?"

"Iggy?" Olivette said, surprised. "What choice did he have—moronic, mean, programmed from birth to think only of survival—it's done, you know? We are all programmed—one way or another. . . . Iggy stupidly believed he had the answers. Imamu, I studied it all—our lives in the bombed-out inner cities, the way we're programmed—like rats. . . ."

"You got a bad habit of confusing things, Olivette," Imamu said, feeling a hot flush rise, burning his body, his neck, his face. "You reduce everything to make things look the way you want."

"Not at all. But you see what is happening—if you want to admit it. That night—that accident—those addicts, robbing victims—taking away anything they could carry—to do what with? To give it back to them—keep the system working. Those sick people could so easily be picked up—and cleaned up—done something with. But they're out there to help keep a sick system working. When too many people start to complain, Imamu, they'll get them. They are programmed to be done away with. So what's wrong with my using Iggy?"

"Man—you're crazy!" Imamu's hair at the back of his neck started rising.

"Crazy?" Olivette kept trying to catch Imamu's eyes. "Are you calling me crazy because I have studied society —this society, and because I'm trying to broaden your understanding of it?"

"Crazy, to use a poor cat like Iggy—then kill him."

"But I didn't. The police did. I just knew how their minds worked. . . ."

"You were the cause of it!"

"No more than you were," Olivette said. "And I don't blame you. You didn't love Iggy. How could you? What was in him to love—although he obviously expected you to love him. His mind was twisted. He was violent. Heavens, Imamu, he had already killed two men. There was nothing about him that could be worked with—to bring about perfection."

"God, Olivette. What you're saying is that you're just like them!"

"Them?"

"Yes, them—the 'thems' and 'theys' you're always talking about. Isn't what you did to Iggy as bad as killing off Indians and putting them on reservations—because they believe in the sun?"

"Imamu," Olivette said, getting angry. "I have no power. I'm a product of the inner city. I'm a child of the 'theys' and 'thems,' put in the inner city because one of my great-grandparents, back there, was black. I didn't create it—I only adjusted to working within it."

"Olivette—man. I can't believe that with all we talked about what you're about is turning our tragedy into your profit."

"Profit?" Olivette almost shouted. Then as Pierre's deep breathing changed, he lowered his voice. "Because I'm trying to perfect a system—to make sure that we're not the only victims . . . ?"

"Words, words, words. Man, I believed them—I believed in you. But there's nothing you can say to make up for—Gladys. . . ."

"Imamu," Olivette said, a puzzled frown pleating his brow. "I never used you—I could have, you know? But I loved you—I wanted to be your friend. . . ."

Imamu ran from the room and down the stairs, needing to put distance between him and Olivette's emotional pleas. He couldn't bear it. He couldn't. "Imamu, come back here," Olivette called down the stairs. "I admit I made a mistake. But I'm only nineteen. I'm still young. . . ."

Imamu heard him but refused to stop. He rushed out into the dark morning running, and running, and running. . . .

19

"And that's the story," Imamu said. He sat at the Aimsleys' kitchen table, drinking coffee, and looking from Peter Aimsley, in his work clothes, to Ann Aimsley, smart in a dark skirt and silk blouse—her going-to-meeting clothes. From the corner of his eye he could see Gail at the kitchen sink, washing dishes. Her small, sharp, intelligent-looking face was prettier than he remembered because of her sunburn.

Strange. He had called when he had left Olivette, to find that she had come back that morning. He must have been psychic to have felt the need to call. And she had to have been psychic, to have come back earlier than she had said. She must have sensed his need for her.

"What a story," Ann Aimsley said. "Inconceivable that a strange child like your Olivette exists. What a horror."

"What intelligence," Gail said. "Fascinating."

"Too much so," Peter Aimsley said wryly. "The devil must have had the same kind of fascination." Imamu's eyes snapped over Peter Aimsley.

"Olivette doesn't believe in the devil. He talked of people, the things they do. . . ."

"That kind never does," Peter Aimsley said.

"Oh, Daddy, stop categorizing everyone—by your values," Gail said, and Imamu wanted to get up and go to her. That's what he missed. A someone who talked like Gail—objectively. He hated admitting that he hadn't missed her as much as he should have—that Olivette had seemed all he wanted—for a time. But then Olivette . . .

"After all, Gail," Ann Aimsley said. "However intelligent he might think he is, he's responsible for Iggy's death, and for Imamu's friend Gladys's—possible death. That's the work of a lunatic."

"Mother," Gail said. "No one is saying that he is completely right. But is it a question of things being merely right or wrong? Isn't it a question of responsibility?"

"Whose?" Peter Aimsley barked.

"Society's," Gail said.

"What cr—aap." Peter Aimsley stood up.

"Mr. Aimsley," Imamu said, a hot flush of anger burning his face. He hated that a man he dug was taking the easiest way out. "Look, I can't even get you to come to visit where I live. And if Gail comes, you suffer a heart attack. You think it's hell. If it is, it was that long before Olivette ever came to live there."

"And will be long after Olivette is gone," Gail said. "But Imamu." She looked at him, grinning. "You are really quite brilliant. How did you ever come to think it was Olivette?"

"Simple," Imamu said, teasing. A thrill of pride rushed through him. "Eliminate the impossible."

"After all," Ann Aimsley said, "Imamu did solve Perk's disappearance. . . ." For a time they sat quietly; then Imamu spoke.

"At first it was just a feeling. You know how it is? You keep hearing things—the radio, the perfect crimes. Olivette drumming the word into my head—perfection, perfection. I guess unconsciously, it began to fit. The perfect Phantom Burglar.

"What started me to thinking was Pierre coming in and making that big slip about Iggy." Imamu thought of Brown, pretending to be looking down at his shoes. He *had* to have heard—and *should* have reacted. "Pierre had to have done it intentionally! God, the first thing I saw turning into that block was Brown's car parked right outside the door. It was shining so bright, nobody could have missed it except by intention. Which meant Pierre came in intending for Brown to get what he wanted— what they both wanted—out of him.

"Then I got to thinking of Iggy. That stud loves to use a knife. He never walks without his. But Gladys's head was beaten with a brick. Auerbach, too, had been beaten. And Gladys? She had to have walked at least part of the way because she wanted to. Gladys wasn't about to walk nowhere with a cat she didn't dig."

"Good, sound thinking," Peter Aimsley said.

"Very logical," Gail agreed.

"But the real reason I nailed it," Imamu said, embarrassed, "had nothing to do with logic." Imamu felt the fool explaining and trying to make Gail believe: "It was this nightmare. I had it twice," he said. "All about a pack of rats—running, getting away from evil—rushing to sure death. And knowing they were rushing to death, I fought to get out. But they kept forcing me. . . . What to do? There I was, so much more intelligent—yet forced on to my death—and couldn't stop it.

"I got up in a sweat. But then I saw. When a dude

goes through a sewer, something's got to rub off on him.
And Olivette's been through many a sewer, in—and out
—of inner cities."

"What about you, Imamu?" Ann Aimsley protested.

"Yeah," Imamu said, reaching for a toothpick.
"That's how I know all about it . . ."

They were all silent, remembering the trouble Imamu
had had with the law. Then Ann Aimsley said, "Nevertheless, it seems to me that you have to to go to the police."

"Who? Me?"

"A boy like that needs help."

"Maybe—but not from the police. . . ."

"That's not for you to decide, Imamu," Peter Aimsley
said. "It's for the courts."

"But I got to decide if I turn him in to the bulls. What
for? So that they can beat his head in? Imprison him?
Not if what he needs is help."

"What's wrong with you going to them and telling
them he needs help? Surely you can't let him stay out on
the streets."

"Mr. Aimsley, you got to know they don't listen to
dudes like me. They don't hardly listen to grown folks,
living in the inner city."

"Well it's about time they did," Peter Aimsley said.

"But they don't," Gail said. "And you know it,
Daddy. Besides, with Imamu's record, and his experi-
ences—you'd hardly expect him to turn in his friend."

"I need help," Imamu said, feeling his helplessness. "Olivette needs your help." He looked at Ann
Aimsley.

"What about his mother?"

"I don't know," Imamu said in anguish. He didn't. He
didn't know what Flame Larouche thought about her

son, his activities. Imamu remembered the way she had stormed into court, in Olivette's defense. But he remembered too the resentment between them. What if she wanted a new life—with Brown . . . ?

"What he needs is someone the law will listen to— someone with status—like a social worker. . . . We need you, Mrs. Aimsley."

"Mother'll help," Gail said. "We all will do whatever we can."

"I can't see him in jail," Imamu said.

"But I can't guarantee that he won't be," Ann Aimsley said.

"You can guarantee that he won't get his head bashed in," Imamu said. "They'll take your recommendation under consideration."

"Can you convince Olivette that it will be the best thing to let me handle it?" Ann Aimsley asked.

"I'll talk to him," Imamu said. "I—we like each other —a lot."

"I got that message," Gail said. "Wasn't Olivette the reason you didn't come to say good-bye?"

"That's a time gone." Imamu grinned. "Just like summer's about to be. . . ."

Imamu left the Aimsleys after breakfast. Walking down the tree-lined street, watching it come to life— workers, young men and women, quick-stepping toward the subway, the middle-aged, getting into their cars, driving off. Women in their bathrobes, watering the gardens of their brownstones, while children sitting at the tops of steps watched, yawning. Imamu hated leaving. He hated the thought of going down into the subway, of taking a trip back to the avenue where he lived, where the junkies stood around, and the winos sat around, where people stood around watching, waiting to be disturbed. At the corner Imamu looked back the length of the block, which the thickly leaved branches of trees blocked, except for the slowly moving feet of women and the water trickling into the gutter.

At home he took a bath, letting his body soak out its tiredness. He hadn't been to sleep since his dream in the early morning. . . . Now, fighting off sleep induced by the hot bath, he dressed. He didn't know Olivette's plans. But he wanted to get to him before he made any.

It was already past eleven when he left his house and made his way up toward Olivette's. Crossing the street, he waved to Al Stacy, busy taking numbers near the corner.

"Hey, Youngblood," Al Stacy called to him, then left his customers to walk to the corner. "Hear the news?"

"What news, man?" Imamu asked, anxious. Around that busy avenue one hour away could make many changes.

"Gladys, man. She's conscious. Her head still done up in bandages but she's gonna make it." Al Stacy pulled up his shoulders, forcing his white jacket to lie flat on his flat stomach.

"I sure am glad," Imamu said, smiling. "You know me and Gladys. . . ."

"Sure, I know. It's been hard on us all. Still, I wish Iggy hadn't gone before I got my hand on him—just for one second. . . ."

"Yeah, well. . . ." Imamu owed nothing to Iggy's memory. Surely not more than he owed to Olivette—and Al Stacy. "Gladys talk to you?"

"Naw, she can't talk, yet. Can't move—except for her eyes. That chick's got some pretty eyes. Oh well, that big mouth of hers gets her in a lot of trouble—more than she can handle." Al Stacy laughed fondly.

"Yeah, sure can," Imamu said, walking away.

The shine of Brown's car, parked in front of the Larouche house, stopped Imamu as he turned into the block. He thought of turning back. What could he talk about to Olivette in front of Brown? He turned away, then decided that he and Olivette could always go out— to the park.

"Hey, Imamu . . . ?" Looking up at the stoop where he had stopped, Imamu saw Furgerson. He looked heavier than Imamu had remembered. Perhaps because his shirt was opened, the buttons all gone. Stepping down the steps in his slippers, Furgerson's heavy stomach hung out over the top of his pants.

"Furgerson! What you doing out here?"

"I quit working," Furgerson said, scratching his big belly, looking lazy.

"Since when?"

"Since last night, man. When I come from work, Iggy was doing his thing. I seen him come tumbling down, man."

"Oh—that was something," Imamu said, getting quiet.

"Sure was," Furgerson said. "So I decided to rest this morning."

"You outa your mind?" Imamu asked. "You give up your good job, just like that? On account of Iggy dying?"

"I took my good job on account of Iggy. So I guess I can quit on account of Iggy," Furgerson said, walking down the stoop in his slippered feet, to stand next to Imamu. "Man," he said. "That's one long trip. Brooklyn? That's another country. I'm tired. Got to catch up on my sleep, man. Get ready for school."

Imamu stood studying his fat friend for a moment. "You tell your boss, you ain't going in?"

"He'll find out soon enough," Furgerson said.

"Go on back upstairs and call him. Tell him you got a refill—will be in early tomorrow."

"Who?"

"Me."

"You? Man, you know how far it is—all the way out to Brooklyn?"

"It ain't far enough," Imamu answered.

Imamu waited, to make sure Furgerson went in, before going down the street to Olivette's. He ran up the steps and was about to ring the bell when he heard: "Jones, where you think you're on your way to?" Looking around, Imamu saw Brown sitting in his car.

"Gonna see the folks," he said.

"They ain't there," Brown said. "They're gone."

"Gone? Where?" Imamu said, ringing the bell, anyway.

"Don't know, Jones. They cleared out—kaput. Landlady let me in. I looked around, and–they–are–gone. . . ."

Imamu came down the steps to stand next to the car. Gone? But he had just left Olivette earlier that morning. He looked at the big man, studied his empty face. With importance blown out of him, Brown looked almost human—unhappily so. Even his moustache seemed to have taken a beating and drooped around his mouth.

What now? Imamu's instant of pain changed to relief. Olivette was gone. Now he could tell Brown. But why? Knowing would scoop out the rest of him. To know that he hadn't solved the case, but was instead a friend—a good friend—of the Phantom Burglar and Gladys's attacker. He might even try to take it out on Imamu. Iggy

was dead. The case was solved. He was free. Let it be.
Let it be.

"Man, sure am sorry to hear that," Imamu said. He
actually did feel sorry for Brown.

"Cut out—just like that?" Brown shook his head in
disbelief. "Didn't even leave a clue. . . ."

But they had. They were off to another inner city,
somewhere, where Flame Larouche could preside in lux-
ury, with the Browns, or some other "lovely man" who
would be a "great influence" on Olivette as they waited
for the next close-call, to move on to another, then another inner city, so amply provided by the "thems," the
"theys". . . .

"Want me to drop you?" Brown asked Imamu.

"Naw, I'm just around the corner."

"Don't matter. It won't take a minute. . . ."

Even the Browns of the world needed company—
someone to cry to. Imamu got into the car. Brown
started it up, his eyes looking out, sad enough for tears,
over his drooping moustache. "I was about ready to give
it up, man," he said, as they drove. "Ready to go all the
way for that lady. . . ."

"Yeah." Imamu nodded understanding. "She sure was
a gone lady."

"A real lady," Brown said. "She comes from one of
them high-class Louisiana Creole families. She ain't
nothing, if she ain't class."

"Where you from, Brown?"

"Louisiana. And I tell you, Jones, if I was back there
—no way I'd have been able to even get near enough to
touch the lady. . . ."

"No jive? Well," Imamu sighed. "Like my boy Olivette says, everything is just about everything, ain't it?"

They waited for the light to change. Brown kept tapping the wheel of the car. "Be seeing you back in court," he said. "Charges will be dropped, of course—against you and Olivette."

"Yeah."

"You know, Jones," Brown said, after a long sigh. "You ain't such a bad boy."

"I been trying to tell you that, Brown. Anyway—thanks, man." The world had to be changing, when a Brown could admit such a thing to an Imamu Jones. He had to be grateful.

Brown drove up and stopped in front of Imamu's building. Looking into the hallway, he said, "So, you got your place all painted up for your old lady?"

"Just about," Imamu said.

"When she coming home?"

"Dunno, maybe in a week—two. . . ."

"Guess she'll be more than a little pleased with you—the place. . . ."

"If she gets around to seeing it."

"How's that?"

"Well, I'm thinking of getting a place away from here—maybe in Brooklyn. A nice section. You see, I'm getting this slave, and I want to be at least running distance from her."

"Hey, that'll be hard on her. She's been living here a long time. She got friends—old friends. . . ."

"She ain't so old she can't make new ones," Imamu said.

"She might hate you for it," Brown said. "Her kind of living, you can't take away from her. Folks get on that cheap rotgut stuff, and they don't change."

"That's not the way I see it, Brown. . . ." Imamu said.

"You see, I got this idea. I'm gonna get it to her—there's such a thing as perfection, see. . . . She's got to get her hand into things—like say, gardening—and prove to herself she can be the most perfect gardener. . . ."

"Jones, it sounds like you think you can remake the world. . . ."

"Well, with a little help from the sun—and rain—and a few other things. . . . Know what I mean . . . ?"

THE FRIENDS

Edith always got to school late, with her clothes unpressed and her holey stockings bagging round her legs. She acted friendly, but Phyllisia didn't want her for a friend – even though, in this strange, hostile city of New York, she badly needed one. Then came the dreadful day when Phyllisia got into a fight . . .

EDITH JACKSON

Orphans always find each other, and that was what happened to seventeen-year-old Edith Jackson. Mrs Bates found her desperately trying to hold the remnants of a family together, and recognized her own past. She had struggled against the handicap of being poor, black, female and an orphan, and she longed for Edith to do the same. But tough, shrewd woman that she was, Mrs Bates knew that until Edith herself decided that she was a person who could make choices and fight for them, she wouldn't begin to count.